Corpses For

Christmas

Nanci M. Pattenden

Corpses for Christmas

Copyright © 2018 Nanci M. Pattenden

This is a work of fiction. All characters, names, incidents, organizations, and dialogue in this novel are either the products of the author's imagination or are used fictitiously.

Published by Murder Does Pay, Ink
Ontario, Canada
www.murderdoespayink.ca

ISBN: 978-1-7750491-1-1 (print)
ISBN: 978-1-7750491-3-5 (Kindle)

1 2 3 4 5 6 7 8 9

ACKNOWLEDGMENTS

I'd like to say a great big thanks to Omar and Ashley, owners of Cardinal Press Espresso Bar in Newmarket for providing a wonderful environment in which to work. They have a lovely big room in the back of their coffee shop, creating the perfect place to call "my office."

As always, thanks to my editor, MJ, of Infinite Pathways, and Chris, my graphics guru.

THANK YOU

TABLE OF CONTENTS

CHAPTER ONE

Detective Albert Hodgins should have been surprised the Christmas reunion with his older brother would turn out to be less than pleasant, but he wasn't. Not really. Jonathan had arrived late Friday evening, December 4 after an exhausting three-day train ride from Boston. The heavy bags under his eyes gave evidence of how little rest he'd managed on the Pullman sleeping car. He'd gone straight to Hodgins' guest room, too tired to have a conversation, an occasional snore the only indication of his presence.

Jonathan stumbled downstairs and into the kitchen just as Albert , Cordelia, and Sara were finishing their breakfast. Cordelia rose to set a place for him, but he waved her off.

"Not now, thank you." He rubbed his belly. "Stomach's still a tad unsettled, what with all the jostling on the train and bad food. Just a cup of tea, if you don't mind."

"Mommy makes the most scrumptious breakfast,"

Sara said, neatly cutting her last piece of sausage and popping it into her mouth.

Jonathan sat beside his brother and looked at the young girl peeking around Albert, smiling. "Why, you must be Sara. I hadn't realized you were such a big girl. My Cora's very excited to meet you."

Not wanting to be left out, Scraps padded over to sniff the intruder. Satisfied he wasn't a threat, he licked Jonathan's hand then went to the back door.

"Sara, put your coat on and take the dog out back." Cordelia turned to Jonathan and Albert, full tea cup in hand. "Take this and the pair of you can go into the sitting room to get reacquainted."

Hodgins refilled his tea cup, grabbed a couple of scones, then ushered his brother down the hall. Jonathan settled back into one of the high-backed wing armchairs by the fire and closed his eyes.

"It's been too long. I should have come back to Toronto for a visit sooner."

"Fault's not all yours. We could have gone down to Boston to see you just as easily. Could have kept up with the correspondence too, I suppose."

"So, it's settled. We're both as bad as each other." Jonathan opened his eyes and nodded at the scones Hodgins had brought in. "Those as good as Sara said?"

"You tell me." He handed one to Jonathan. Half of it disappeared in one bite.

"What was it she said? Scrumptious? I agree. Maybe I can manage a bit of breakfast after all."

Hodgins lifted the plate, extending it to Jonathan. "Here, have the other one. Now, tell me what this business deal you came early for is all about."

Jonathan stuffed the scone in his mouth and washed it down with some tea. "Oh, it's nothing, really. Possibility of a new shipping contract. Captain won't be back in Boston for a few months and I wanted to settle it before he sails back to the England." He hesitated, tearing a chunk out of the last scone. Jonathan popped it into his mouth, then washed it down with the rest of his tea. "Truth be told, I wanted a bit of time to myself. Elizabeth's been talking about this trip for weeks, and it's become somewhat tiresome. I also wanted to speak with you without the family around."

Hodgins sensed Jonathan wanted to discuss something other than old times. "What's troubling you brother?"

Jonathan stared at the fire and shrugged. "Just wanted to talk to my brother, that's all."

Hodgins wasn't convinced, but he remembered how difficult it'd been growing up to get Jonathan to say anything before he was ready. "Stubborn as ever."

Jonathan opened his mouth to reply, but a knock on the front door stopped him.

"Who the devil comes calling unannounced on a Saturday?" Hodgins grumbled. "Can't be good news."

Jonathan laughed. "When is an unexpected knock on a police officer's door ever good news?"

Hodgins set his teacup on the floor beside his chair before getting up. "In my experience, practically never."

Snow rode in on the back of a cold wind as he opened the front door. A constable he didn't recognize stood on the front porch, hopping up and down, trying to stay warm. He stopped when he saw Detective Hodgins.

"Sir, they've found a body and you've been requested."

"Haven't seen you before. Must be new. Step in out of the cold."

"Constable Perry, sir. Thank you, sir."

"Now what's this about me being asked for?"

"Asked for you special. Headmaster's request."

Hodgins was puzzled. "Headmaster? Whatever are you going on about, Constable?"

"Ketchum School, sir. Grounds-keeper found a body this morning. In the school yard. Headmaster said he knows you. Demanded no one should touch nothing 'til you've been fetched."

"Fine. Tell them I'll be along shortly." Hodgins shut the door behind the constable and turned to find his brother standing in the doorway of the sitting room. "Damn. Take one day off to visit with my brother and it lasts…" He glanced at the hall clock. "All of two hours."

"Who was that?"

"Harry, or was it Perry? Got a batch new of recruits last week." Hodgins shrugged. "Can't get their names straight. Most of them probably won't last the month. Someone found a body at Sara's school and sent for me. Why the devil would someone leave a body in the school yard?" He shook his head and sighed. "A day off is frequently never a complete day off."

The detective removed his overcoat from the peg and walked down the hall to the kitchen door. Cordelia stood at the window watching Sara playing with Scraps.

"Delia,"—he chuckled when she jumped, always amused at how easily she startled. "I've been called out. Jonathan's decided he's able to eat after all. I know the dishes have been washed and put away, but would you mind fixing him something?"

She put her hands on her hips, her Irish temper surfacing. "Albert Hodgins, are you suggesting I'd be put out to prepare a meal for your only brother?"

7

He took a step back, waving his hands. "No, not at all. Won't be long."

As he passed his brother, Albert made him promise not to mention where the body had been found. "I'll tell her myself when I know more. You may as well use the time to get reacquainted with Cordelia."

Hodgins slipped into his overcoat, buttoning it as he made his way down the hall.

Last night's heavy snowfall made the trek to Ketchum School slow. At least it was only about four blocks away. A few people were out taking care of their Saturday errands, the wagons and buggies leaving ruts in the snow, along with a few deposits from the horses. Hodgins walked on the road, following the buggy tracks as much as possible, carefully avoiding the dung. By the time he reached the school, the dampness from the snow had crept almost to the knees of his trousers. The wet pants clung to his legs, causing him to shiver. Headmaster Gruger rushed over to greet him.

"Detective Hodgins, thank heavens you're here. This is terrible, just terrible. Can you imagine if the children were here? Oh, no, that would be utterly terrible. Why would someone leave a body here?"

Gruger wrung his hands and looked back towards the constable and grounds-keeper standing near the body.

Hodgins surveyed the area while the headmaster blathered on. He jumped in as soon as Gruger stopped for a breath.

"Why did you ask for me?"

Gruger looked shocked. "Your daughter is a student here. I assumed you'd want to deal with this personally."

"Yes, of course. I understand. Don't some of the children normally play around here on the weekend? I'm surprised they aren't making snowmen or having a snowball fight. We'll work as quickly as we can. Wouldn't want a child coming across the body. Disturbing sight, even for an adult. Do you know the victim? Does he work here?"

Gruger shook his head. "Haven't seen him before. We'd never hire someone as rough looking as that chap. Please, can you move him now? With all this snow the children are sure to be here soon. As you said, the field makes for a splendid place to build forts and have a snowball fight."

The more Hodgins thought about the location of the corpse the more anxious he was to find out what happened. If there was a murderer hanging around the school, maybe he'd keep Sara home for a few days.

"Why don't you go inside Headmaster? Get out of the snow and cold." Hodgins turned to the constable that dragged him from his nice warm house. "Has the coroner been called?"

"Yes, sir. Another constable went right away. Should be here soon."

"Right," Hodgins said. "What have you found out so far?" He glanced at Gruger's back. The headmaster walked slowly, reluctant to leave. "Don't suppose you recognize the dead man?"

The constable indicated he didn't as they walked over to the body. The area was covered in about a foot of freshly fallen snow, obliterating any indication of the direction the victim and murderer came from. The body sat propped up against the brick wall of the school, a bloody handkerchief tied around his head. It had slipped and the right eye peeked over the top, staring but not seeing. The snow around the body was tinted pink from blood, and one woolen sock stuck out from under the corpse. Hodgins crouched down beside the dead body and surveyed the school yard.

"Look from this angle, Harry." He motioned for the constable to kneel. "The snow is laying smooth and undisturbed everywhere except there." Hodgins pointed toward the treed area to the south. "It looks rough, as though the new snow covered a path where someone trod."

"It's Perry, sir." He crouched down beside Hodgins

and nodded. "Suppose so, sir."

As Hodgins started to respond to the new recruit, the sound of bells caught his attention. He turned his head and watched a wagon approach, silver bells glistening along the harness. "Looks like the coroner is here and ready for the holidays. Why don't we get out of his way?"

McKenzie greeted Hodgins with a jolly hello and smile, then nodded towards the constable. Hodgins was on friendly terms with both Dr. Hamish McKenzie and his wife. McKenzie groaned as he knelt down beside the body, both knees cracking; first the left, then the right. The sound carried in the stillness of the morning.

"Getting too old and too fat to do this," he muttered. He looked up at Hodgins. "Want to talk to you later. Will you be in your office this afternoon?"

"Hope not. It's my day off. I'd like to get back home, if at all possible. What can you tell us about this poor chap?"

"I assume you've noticed he has a handkerchief tied around his head, covering his eyes? Well, almost covering his eyes. Looks like it used to be white."

"Stop stating the obvious, Doctor," Hodgins said as he smiled.

McKenzie lifted the lower edge of the hanky but didn't try to remove it. "There's a bullet lodged over his left eye. Just the tip is poking through the skin. No wounds anywhere else that I can see." He lifted the flat cap perched on the man's head. "Correction. Blood here, on top of his head." He dropped the hat back down, and lifted the hands one at a time, examining them carefully. "No signs of a struggle or attempt to fight off whoever did this."

McKenzie put one hand on the school wall and grunted again as he slowly got to his feet. "If you don't need me for anything else, I'll take him back and examine him and his clothing inside where it's warm. If someone wouldn't mind helping carry him to my wagon, I'll get started."

Perry and the grounds-keeper carried the corpse over, dropping him in the back hard enough to bounce the wagon and startle the horse.

"Little more care if you please. He may be dead, but he deserves to be treated with some respect. Is that how you'd want your body handled after you pass?"

"No, Doctor," Perry mumbled.

The grounds-keeper just turned and walked back towards the school, totally ignoring the doctor's question.

"There's not much more I can do until we hear back from the coroner. Snow's pretty much covered any possible evidence," Hodgins told the constable. "Ask the grounds-keeper if he has a shovel you can use. Clear away some of the snow. See if anything dropped in it. I'll be at home if you find something significant."

"Shovel snow?" the recruit asked. "Doesn't seem like something a copper should do."

Hodgins glared at him. "If you plan on staying employed with the Toronto Constabulary, you'll bloody well do what you're told, without moaning. There's a lot more unpleasant things you'll be doing, so think yourself lucky it's only snow."

The young man stared at Hodgins for a moment, mouth open. After mumbling an apology, he scurried after the grounds-keeper.

Hodgins took one last look around before heading down the laneway to Scollard and back to his home on Lowther.

As he passed McKenzie's wagon, the coroner reminded him he wanted to have a chat. "Why don't you and your wife join us for your evening meal? Say seven o'clock?" Hodgins asked. "You can meet my brother."

"Splendid idea. Looking forward to it. Seven it is."

* * *

Scraps came racing down the hall as soon as the front door opened. Even though the dog had been given to Sara as a birthday gift, it was quite attached to Hodgins. Leaning against the door, Hodgins braced for the impact. The scrawny stray had turned into a large, affectionate, but fiercely protective dog. His head banged back on the door when the dog jumped. Scraps' front paws planted firmly on Hodgins' chest, pinning him to the door.

"Down boy. Let me get my coat off." He gently pushed the dog away and brushed the snow from his overcoat before hanging it on the peg.

"I see you've got that beast well trained," Jonathan joked. "I hope you can teach him some manners before Elizabeth arrives with the children. Much as she like dogs, I don't think she'd appreciate being knocked over by him."

"Don't worry. Your wife will be quite safe. He only does that to me. Don't know if I should be pleased or insulted." He caught a whiff of the aroma wafting down the hall from the kitchen. Cabbage soup. "Smells like I've arrived in time for lunch."

Hodgins and his brother went into the kitchen, Scraps trotting ahead, leading the way.

"Soup will be ready in about twenty minutes," Cordelia said. She looked her husband up and down. "Why don't you get out of those wet things before you catch your death."

"Yes, dear. Oh, we're having company tonight. Dr. McKenzie wants to talk to me about something. It sounded important so I invited him and his wife to dine with us. Hope you don't mind."

Cordelia wiped her hands on a towel, draping it over the back of a chair as she moved to her husband. She took Hodgins' suit jacket, hanging it on the back of a chair near the wood stove. "Not at all. You know I love any excuse to have a party, even a small one. And I haven't seen Morag in quite some time. It's short notice, but I've plenty of time to prepare. Now go put something dry on."

He snatched two of the cooling scones and tossed one at his brother on his way out of the kitchen.

* * *

"That was a splendid meal, Cordelia." Dr. McKenzie smacked his lips and rubbed his belly. "You're a wonderful cook."

"Thank you, Hamish. I'm so glad you and Morag could join us. We don't see you near often enough."

"Afraid it won't be any more often in the future. That's what I want to talk to you about Albert."

Morag rose and joined Cordelia at the sink. "I'll help you and Sara clear while the men have their little chat, and I'll tell you all about it."

Hodgins, Jonathan and Hamish retired to the sitting room and Hodgins poured them each a whisky.

"OK, you've got my full attention, Hamish. What's

on your mind?"

"If you wish to speak in private, I can take the dog for a walk," Jonathan said.

McKenzie shook his head. "No, nothing confidential. Stay in where it's warm." The doctor turned back to Albert. "Wanted to tell you personally, before you hear it from someone else. On Monday I'll be handing in my notice. These old bones just can't take it much longer."

"Then we'll be seeing more of you, not less."

"Afraid not. We're moving back to Scotland. My sister isn't well and I'd like to spend some time with her before … well, you understand."

Hodgins glanced over at his brother. "Yes, I understand what it's like to be separated from family. At least my brother is only a train ride away. A rather long ride, but fortunately we're on the same continent. I'll be sorry to see you go. We'll have to throw you one heck of a wing-ding. Send you off proper."

"How long has it been since you've seen your sister?" Jonathan asked.

"Ach, longer than I'd care to admit. I've only been back home once since moving to Canada. Our children are grown with families of their own. My eldest boy is in Australia, of all places. Professor at the University of Sydney, teaching chemistry. Me and the missus are too old to travel much. Figure if the children are going to be travelling to visit us, they can come over to Scotland to do it just as easily as coming here.

* * *

Despite Cordelia's protests, Morag took the towel from Sara and dried the dishes as Cordelia washed them.

"We can chat easier this way," Morag said.

Cordelia smiled and asked Sara to finish clearing the table.

"Such a lovely child," Morag commented, as Sara placed the dirty dishes by her mother, then put away the dried ones.

Sara blushed, then moved across the room. She knelt down by the wood stove to scratch Scrap's head, listening as her mother and Mrs. McKenzie chatted while finishing up the dishes.

"We've been away from Scotland far too long. I miss everyone. My younger brother and his family don't live too far from Hamish's sister, so I'll be able to visit both often. They've found us a small cottage right around the corner. I just wish we were going under better circumstances."

"Does your husband have any other family?" Cordelia asked.

"No, just the one sister. She stood with me at the wedding all those decades ago. We became fast friends the moment Hamish introduced us. She never married. When we found out she was ill, I wrote my brother. His whole family has been helping out when they can, and my nieces have been doing a lot of the cleaning and cooking this last month or so. She's gotten so much worse recently and may not be able to live on her own much longer. I'm so afraid we may not arrive in time." Mrs. McKenzie wiped her eyes with the corner of the towel. "Gracious, I don't know what came over me."

Cordelia put down her wash rag and took the towel from Morag, replacing it with her own lace handkerchief. "Sit. You must be terribly upset. I can only imagine how you're feeling."

"It's all so overwhelming. We have to pack or sell everything, and Hamish will have to find a replacement coroner. All I can think about is poor Elspeth. She was such a free spirit. Full of life. The last letter from my sister-in-law painted a bleak picture of a total stranger. So frail and completely dependent on them.

"Ahem."

They turned to find Albert and Hamish standing in the doorway. The doctor held his wife's lamb-wool coat and muff.

"It's time we were heading home, my dear. We've lots to do still and it's getting late. Beside, the good detective has to start planning our bon voyage party." He winked at Hodgins. "You can save the tears for then."

His voice softened as he went over and helped her on with her coat. "Everything will be fine. We'll have plenty of time with her. You'll see."

CHAPTER TWO

After church the next day, Hodgins kissed Cordelia and Sara, then hailed a hansom cab to take him to the station house. It was much too cold to walk across the city. A wool blanket sat neatly folded on the seat so he draped it over his legs for warmth. It matched the larger one over the back of the horse.

When he arrived at the station house he was relieved to discover no new major crimes needing his attention. He just settled behind his desk when Constable Barnes popped in.

"Sir, I'm glad you're here. The Inspector has been asking for you. He's quite agitated."

"What now? It's been pretty quiet lately. We've no high-profile cases at the moment, just one unidentified corpse. Don't suppose the inspector told you anything?"

"No, but the desk sergeant did. Seems someone came in late yesterday afternoon." Barnes flipped open his notebook and checked the last entry. "Man by the name of Gruger."

Hodgins groaned. "He's the headmaster at Sara's school."

"Is Sara in some sort of trouble?"

"No, some fool went and got himself murdered. That corpse I mentioned. Surprised you haven't heard about it. I'll check in with the inspector then fill you in. Don't go far. I have a feeling we're going to be busy."

* * *

An hour later Hodgins returned from the inspector's office. As he passed an empty desk, he shoved the chair out of the way, with considerably more force than necessary.

"Barnes, my office." Hodgins slammed the door after he entered. A moment later Barnes eased the door open and slipped in, closing it gently behind him.

"Sir?"

Hodgins paced behind his desk.

"You know how much I dislike politics? Well, Gruger, the headmaster at Sara's school, has gone to the Chief Inspector and insisted not only that I personally handle this, but to keep him informed of our progress. The Chief gave our Inspector a right earful, which he passed on to me. He blathered on and on. I thought I'd never get out of there."

Barnes cocked his head to the side, a puzzled look on

his face. "Sir? Progress on what?"

"What? Oh, sorry." Hodgins waved his hand towards the chair in front of his desk. "Sit. Got so worked up I forgot I hadn't filled you in." He stopped pacing long enough to let Barnes know what had happened on his so-called day off.

"It's that unidentified corpse. Someone left a body leaning up against Ketchum School. One of those new constables dragged me from my nice warm house to look into it. Wish they'd open up a station house in my neighbourhood. The city's growing and we have to keep up."

"Not much need for one up in St. Paul's Ward yet. Most of the north end is brick and tile yards or open space. East side's still sparsely populated. Your home is in the only area with a proper neighbourhood."

Hodgins finally sat. "True. Lots of homes on the west side, but it's still fairly quiet. A nice neighbourhood, as you well know."

He noticed Barnes colour slightly at the indirect mention of the pretty, young neighbour Barnes was sweet on.

"One good thing about this case – it's not far from home. I can check on the site and question the people who live around the school either on the way to work or the way home."

The faint smile disappeared as he thought about the location.

"Just wish it hadn't happened at Sara's school. Or any school for that matter. Not something I'd want any of the children to find, even though it wasn't too gruesome." A huge grin spread across his face. "I think you would've been able to handle that one."

Barnes turned bright red.

"Don't worry lad. I don't believe everyone knows you've puked at two murder scenes this year. New recruits haven't been told, yet." Hodgins couldn't hold back his laughter.

Barnes sat straight, pulling his shoulder back. "Seen my fair share since then, sir. I'm used to anything now."

Hodgins doubted someone so young could harden up after only a year, but he didn't say so.

"No need to be embarrassed because you have compassion. Just try to hide it better."

"Yes, sir."

"Get your coat and scarf. We need to get over to the school and have a good look around. Seems the headmaster didn't go inside out of the way after all. Just went around the corner of the building, then came back to watch after I left. Nosey old prat. Apparently, Gruger told the Chief Inspector that the constable cleared a large area of snow and only briefly looked through it. The Chief lectured our Inspector on procedure and the training of new recruits. Track down"—Hodgins flipped through his notes—"Perry. Find out why he hasn't submitted a report. I'll have a little talk with Sergeant Evans later and make sure he stresses the importance of speedy reporting to that new batch of nitwits we've got. No one enjoys the paperwork, but it needs to be done while it's fresh in the mind."

They were half-way to the front door when McKenzie limped in. Hodgins raised an eyebrow.

"Whatever happened to you, Doctor?"

"Arthritis is bothering me. Kneeling in the snow Saturday didn't help. Stiffened right up. Like I said, getting too old for this. Need to loosen up my knee, so I thought I'd save you a trip to my morgue. I have my preliminary findings and the man's belongings. Spent all morning examining him. Found something in his pocket you'd be interested in." He handed Hodgins a small card. "It's never easy with you, is it?" McKenzie chuckled.

"What the blazes? How…? I don't understand."

Barnes peered over Hodgins' shoulder. "Oh my. Why would the dead man have your brother's business card?"

"That's a very good question, Constable. I wish I

knew the answer. Jonathan hasn't been back to Toronto for over ten years. Came in Friday on the last train. Picked him up at the station myself."

"To continue," McKenzie said, "I can't give you a positive time of death. Difficult to say what with it being so cold, but my best guess is he was shot sometime Friday evening, probably early evening based on the partially digested meal in his stomach."

"I suppose I'll have to ask Jonathan to come down and look at the body. Maybe he can identify him. Could the dead man also have come in from Boston? What can you tell me about the wound?"

"Single shot through the back of the head. Bullet entered the right side about an inch from the ear and lodged over the left eye. Looks like a .45. There was blood and serum under the scalp on the top of the head. Bits of wood too. I'd say he was bashed on the head with a club of some sort. Can't tell which wound came first, but the bullet was the cause of death." He handed Barnes a small bag. "Contents of his pockets." He smiled and whistled as he exited the station.

"May as well see what's in the bag before we leave. Empty it on that desk and let's have a look." Hodgins took a couple of steps toward an empty desk, Barnes close behind.

Barnes unfolded the top of the bag and tipped it over. A few coins rolled across the desk, stopping at the edge. A red hanky with frayed edges followed the coins, and a folded envelope came halfway out. Barnes reached in and pulled it the rest of the way. The only other items were a pocket watch and a single woolen sock.

"There's something inside the envelope," Barnes said. He unfolded it and lifted the flap. "Sir, look at this." He handed the envelope to Hodgins.

"That's a fair bit of money. Couldn't have been a robbery. Even though the pocket watch isn't expensive, a robber could have got something for it from one of the City's less than upstanding pawnbrokers. Both the watch and money would have been quick enough to grab and run." Hodgins counted the money. "There's fifty dollars here. Why would a thief murder someone and leave so much money behind? And the sock. I saw it sticking out under his leg. How did a sock get under the body? He was wearing shoes, and I'm certain he had socks on both feet." He put everything back inside the bag, except the red hanky. "If this was in his pocket, whose hanky was tied around his eyes?"

Barnes pointed to the business card. "What about that?"

Hodgins thought about it for a few minutes, flipping

it through his fingers. "Did I tell you Gruger was an old school mate of Chief Inspector Paulson? I may have been ordered to keep Gruger informed, but I'm not about to tell him my brother may be involved. Not yet."

He stuffed the hanky inside the bag before pushing it across the desk. "Log this as evidence, then we'll go check the area around the school."

Barnes picked up the small bag, but didn't move.

"Something wrong constable?"

"Don't you want me to log that, too?" Barnes pointed to the card Hodgins still fidgeted with.

"Need to speak with my brother about this. Why don't you just enter it as a business card on the evidence list?"

"Yes sir," Barnes said softly. "Whatever you think is best." He avoided looking Hodgins in the eye.

Barnes turned to go back to his desk, but Hodgins stopped him. The look of disappointment on the constable's face was too much.

"Put down Jonathan's name. I'm sure it's all quite simple to explain. Can't be showing favouritism now, can we?"

Barnes smiled. "No sir. Law's the law."

* * *

"Looks like the children had one heck of a snowball fight."

27

Barnes placed his hands on his hips. "And they've destroyed the entire area."

Footprints riddled the park beside Ketchum School along with smashed snowballs, and the remnants of two snow walls. A few children had arrived to play after changing out of their Sunday best. Hodgins went over to the boy who looked to be the oldest.

"Were you here yesterday, young man?"

"Yes, sir. Is it true then? Heard tell a man was murdered right here in this very park." He was wide-eyed and full of excitement. Hodgins remembered being afraid of nothing at that age.

"Unfortunately. Do you think you can assist us?" The other children had crowded around Hodgins and Barnes, anxious to hear all the gruesome details. "I'm sorry, but I can't tell you very much. Ongoing investigation, but maybe you can help us solve it."

All the boys bobbed their heads in agreement, the few girls with them stood back a bit, except one. She looked to be about seven or eight. The girl spoke up.

"My uncle is with the North-West Mounted Police. He told us always to help whenever we can. Not even wait to be asked." She stood with her arms crossed as though waiting to be told to be quiet, with a look that suggested she was more than willing to fight anyone who tried to stop her.

"North-West Mounted Police? Impressive." Hodgins had heard about the new force established the previous year on the advice of Prime Minister MacDonald. "And what's your name?"

"Sally French." She uncrossed her arms and leaned forward. "Are you really going to let us help?"

"Yes, Sally. I'm really going to let you help. Were you all here yesterday?"

A chorus of *yeses* echoed around the circle of children.

"Can you help us search among the trees over there? You have to be careful and go very slow. And don't touch anything. If you find something, yell. Either Constable Barnes or myself will come to you."

The children ran across the park to the trees. "Slow and careful now! Hodgins hollered after them.

"Sir, they're children. Shouldn't they be sent home?"

"Do you want to spend all day in the cold, looking through the woods?"

Barnes grinned. "No."

"Right. You look over there and I'll start at this end."

Hodgins recalled the uneven trail that seemed to lead to the body and he followed in that general direction. Little Sally was looking in that area and yelled as Hodgins approached. A tree branch about two feet long and a

Nanci M. Pattenden

couple of inches thick lay in the snow. It was near the edge of the woods, and there was a sticky patch of something coppery-red on it.

"Barnes, over here."

All the children came running, beating Barnes to the spot.

Barnes bent over, resting his hands on his knees, huffing and puffing.

"You're out of shape, Constable. We'll never win that hockey game against Station House One if all my officers are in such bad condition. We'll have to set up a training schedule."

"Yes… sir." Barnes took a few more deeps breaths.

"Is that wot killed him?" One of the boys asked. They had enclosed Hodgins in a circle, straining to see what was in the snow.

"Could be. Look around and see if you can spot anything else. And remember, if you find something, don't touch it."

"What is it? What did the little girl find?" Barnes asked.

"Remember McKenzie found wood chips in the wound on the victim's head? I think this may be what caused it." Hodgins picked it up and handed it to Barnes

After an hour of searching, nothing more was found,

30

so Hodgins dismissed the children. "Thank you all for your assistance. You can run along now."

"Aw, do we hafta?" one boy asked. A disappointed groan from all the children echoed through the trees before they slowly made their way back to the half-destroyed snow fort.

Hodgins noticed Sally hadn't joined the rest of the children in the park.

"What's your name?" she asked.

"Detective Hodgins."

"Oh, I've heard Grampa talk about you. Says you're very smart. Wait 'till tell him I helped you."

Barnes laughed as Sally ran off, presumably home to tell her grandpa. "You're famous, sir."

"Did she say her name was French? Isn't that the name of the Commissioner of the North-West Mounted Police? Couldn't be the same family, could it? She said her uncle was with the North-West, but French is a fairly common name."

Barnes shrugged.

Hodgins pointed to the branch the constable held. "You get that back to Dr. McKenzie. See if he has any way to determine if it's the same wood as the chips he found. Take a hansom cab. When you get back here, start talking to the neighbours along Berryman. I'll start on Davenport

Road."

Barnes went in search of a cab, holding the branch with both hands. Hodgins walked up the road and knocked on the door of the first house. A lady who looked to be in her forties answered the door.

"Who's there, Ma?" The voice sounded like it came from down the hall.

"I'm Detective Hodgins." He raised his voice so both the lady and her son could hear. "Need to ask a few questions."

A young man came out of one of the rooms in back and joined them. He smiled and extended his hand to the detective. His mother seemed nervous, looking from her son to the detective repeatedly.

"What brings the law out on such a cold day? And a detective at that?" the young man asked.

"Unfortunately, someone was murdered by the school. Did either of you see or hear anything Friday evening? A gun shot perhaps?"

"Oh my!" The lady exclaimed. She fanned herself with her hands.

"Didn't mean to upset you, Mrs.?"

"Perkins," the young man filled in. "I'm her son, Daniel." He turned to his mother. "Go sit down, Ma. I'll take care of this."

Daniel waited until his mother had gone towards the back of the house before answering Hodgins' question.

"No, Detective. We didn't hear anything like that. We were together, having a quiet night. My mother was making a list of things she needs to do to prepare for Christmas. My sister and her family will be arriving in a few weeks. I was reading the newspaper, catching up on the events. All in all, a rather dull evening."

"Thank you for your time. Here's my card, in case you remember something. Anything."

Daniel read the card. "Isn't this a little out of your territory? Station Four is clear across town."

"Sounds like you're familiar with us, Mr. Perkins."

Daniel laughed. "Not me personally. Some of my friends. Little to much too drink at times. Nothing serious."

Hodgins' thought it peculiar that Daniel would be aware of the location of the stations, but he let it pass. "Unusual circumstances, as I said. Contact me if you remember anything."

"Now that I think about it, there was one thing. Heard two men yelling. Didn't last long."

"What time was that?" Hodgins dug his notebook and pencil out of his overcoat pocket.

"Can't rightly say. A bit after we dined. I'd guess

maybe eight or nine o'clock. It was off in the distance so I didn't bother looking out the window."

Hodgins jotted it down, thanked Mr. Perkins, then continued on to the neighbour's. He'd only made it to five houses when Barnes arrived back.

"Doctor McKenzie said he'd try his best to identify the wood. Any luck, sir?"

"Man at number four said he heard some yelling but so far none of the other neighbours heard it. One man thought he might have heard a gunshot, though. Couldn't be positive what it was, as they were singing and playing music."

"I'll check with them people over there." Barnes pointed to Berryman Street. "Maybe they heard or seen something."

"Make sure your notes have proper grammar, Constable."

Barnes look confused, then realized what he'd said. "Yes sir. Sorry sir."

"You're one of the few constables with a proper education. Don't try to hide it. Off with you now."

Barnes nodded and ran up the street. Hodgins detoured to Bishop Street, but no one there admitted to hearing anything. The house on the corner was empty so he jotted a note to remind himself to come back another day before continuing up Davenport. The elderly couple at number sixteen invited him in for tea and biscuits. Hodgins was never one to turn down a hot beverage and food, especially on a day so cold. The elderly lady ushered him into a small room with a roaring fire and four over-stuffed and over-used chairs.

"Have a seat, young man. Let me take your coat." She had the coat off his back before Hodgins could protest, then she pushed him towards one of the chairs. "Sit, please. I insist."

Hodgins sank down and found the chair surprisingly comfortable. The elderly lady scurried off while her husband sat in the chair opposite him, smiling.

"I'm Harold Cotter, by the way. Mable will be back shortly with a little snack. Do you have children Detective?"

Before Hodgins could answer, Harold continued. "We have seven children, fifteen grandchildren, and two great-grandchildren."

Hodgins grinned as he pictured the short, stocky couple surrounded by a family of little chubby grandchildren. He was spared further details when Mable returned with a tray laden with a tea pot, a stack of cups, and biscuits. Before either had the opportunity to start talking again, Hodgins told them what he was there for.

Mrs. Cotter sat the tray on a small table, broke open a biscuit releasing a column of steam, then smothered it with jam and placed it on the saucer before handing Hodgins his tea. His mouth watered. He took a bite and listened as the couple started up again.

"Oh, I told you Harold. Those two were up to no good."

CHAPTER THREE

Hodgins quickly swallowed his biscuit as the Cotters argued about the men she'd mentioned.

"They looked shifty," Mable said.

"Nonsense. They were simply walking down the street."

"But they walked shifty."

"Oh, pshaw. No such thing as walking shifty."

Hodgins interrupted. "What two men?"

"Why those two beggars." She lowered her voice. "One was a negro."

"Martha, no need to whisper. It's not a crime to be a negro. You don't know anything about them. I've met a lot of beggars who were the nicest people you'd ever want to meet. Why just last year—"

Hodgins cut him off. "What can you tell me about the two men?" He took another bite of the biscuit before it cooled. It practically melted in his mouth. Distracted by the biscuit, he missed what Harold said. "Could you repeat that, please?"

"Like Martha said, two men. One like us, the other a negro fellow. I'd say both were middle aged, but can't say for certain. Only saw them from the window, and it was quite dark out, what will the clouds and all."

Hodgins balanced the tea cup and saucer on his knee while writing in his notebook. Fearing he was about to spill the contents, he looked for a spot to place his cup. The small table Mable had placed the tray on sat in the centre of the grouping of chairs, but it was a stretch for him to reach. He decided to set his cup on the floor beside his chair.

"Did you hear any arguing or gunshots Friday evening? Say around eight or nine?"

"Gracious no. We were asleep by nine. Take more than a gunshot to rouse us before morning. Up before the birds, we are. Early to bed, and all that," Harold said.

Since nothing else could be learned from them, Hodgins helped himself to another biscuit with jam before leaving. None of the other residents on the street heard or saw anything. He met up with Barnes an hour after leaving the Cotter's and discovered a few of the people Barnes spoke to also mentioned the two beggars.

"Do you think it might have been them?" Barnes asked. "Several people saw them Friday evening about the time Dr. McKenzie thinks the man was shot."

"Could be. We need to find them and see what they have to say. If it was them, why kill him? Nothing seems to have been taken. Why leave all that money behind?"

"Maybe they were looking for something specific. Not concerned about the money."

"I suppose anything's possible."

Hodgins and Barnes headed back to the station house. The wind whipped the heavy snow around, stinging their faces, so Hodgins flagged down the first hansom he saw. Unfortunately this one didn't have a lap blanket for the customers but at least they were protected. The wind ripped the folding cab door from Barnes' hand just before it shut. Hodgins laughed when Barnes almost fell out trying to grab the door. The trap door on top of the cab slid open and the driver called down.

"Where to, gentlemen?"

"Station House Four," Hodgins answered, and the door slid shut.

"I'll have the driver drop you off so you can fill out a report about the two beggars, then I'll continue to the morgue to see if McKenzie had any luck with that tree branch," Hodgins said.

The trip across Toronto was slow. At Carlton and Jarvis, two carriages blocked the road, right in front of St. Andrew's Church. Their wheels locked, apparently when one of the drivers passed too close to the other carriage. Hodgins leaned back and closed his eyes, listening to the men yell and cuss. Eventually the two rigs were separated and everyone resumed their journeys. Another blast of wind assaulted them when they arrived at the station and Barnes opened the cab door. He fought to keep control of it as he exited, so Hodgins reached over to help. Snow blew in before they got the door shut. Hodgins brushed the flakes away and rapped on the roof of the cab. "Morgue, please."

The driver snapped the reins and continued on. When they arrived, Hodgins paid the fair, pulled up his collar, and ran into the morgue, almost slipping on the front steps. McKenzie sat at his desk, writing. He looked up when he heard the door open

"Just writing out my resignation. First order of business tomorrow. Suppose you're here about the branch young Barnes brought in."

He put the letter in a drawer and indicated for Hodgins to follow him to a table where a microscope sat.

"Take a look."

Hodgins leaned over and looked through the eye piece. "OK, what am I looking at?"

"Bits of wood found in the skull." He changed slides. "This is from the piece Barnes brought in. Notice any similarities?"

Hodgins shrugged. McKenzie put a third slide under the microscope lens. "Now do you see any difference?

"Yes. The spots are spaced farther apart."

"Pores. That one is maple. Now look at the other two again."

Hodgins carefully changed the slides, going back and forth between them. "The spots, er, pores, are a lot smaller and closer together on the sample from the branch and skull."

"Yes. I believe they're both from mountain ash. It's not an exact science, but I'm more than reasonably certain the wood bits in the scalp match the branch. Are the bits in the scalp from that specific branch? No way to be sure, but the blood on it would indicate a connection."

"Thank you, Doctor. I'll take this branch back and mark it as evidence. As you say, no way to be sure, but it was found near the body. At least I was correct about the coppery substance being blood."

"You've got a well-trained eye. And I have a little surprise you'll be happy about. There were some hairs caught under the bark. Same colour and texture as the dead man's. Again, no way to be certain, but I'm confident this was used to club him."

* * *

Hodgins dropped the branch on Barnes' desk as soon as he returned from the morgue.

"Log this as evidence. It's not the murder weapon, but it was likely used to bash the poor chap on the head. Hopefully he was unconscious before being shot. Can you fetch me that envelope?"

Barnes took the branch then joined Hodgins in his office a few minutes later, envelope in hand. Barnes pointed to the printing in the corner of it. "Campbell, Hugh & Son, Ropemaker, Aurora. A pay envelope maybe?"

"Fifty dollars is a rather large wage, don't you think, Constable?"

Barnes nodded in agreement. "Would you like me to fetch the train schedule?"

Hodgins laughed. "You know me well, but no, not yet. Hopefully my brother can tell me who we have in the morgue." He hesitated. "Maybe you should have it handy in the morning, just in case."

* * *

Hodgins and his brother retired to the sitting room after supper, leaving Cordelia and Sara clearing up. "Sara's quite excited to meet your daughter. If she has her way, she'll be dragging Cora all over the city."

"Cora's excited too. Been asking all sorts of

questions. For some reason she's expecting Toronto to be quite different from Boston. Thinks it's all wilderness up here," Jonathan said.

"Hmm, yes. I suppose it will be a little different, but I'm afraid she's going to be disappointed if she's expecting to see bears roaming the streets."

Hodgins pulled out his police notebook and Jonathan glanced at it.

"You were quiet all through supper, Albert. What's on your mind?"

"I have to ask you something. It's about the man found at the school."

"Me? What could I possibly know that would be of any help? I haven't been back in Toronto for over ten years."

Hodgins slipped the card out of his notebook and handed it to Jonathan.

"We found this in his pocket. He was shot sometime early Friday evening. You arrived late Friday night. How did he get your card?"

"I told you, I relocated my premises last year. The address here is the old one on Stillman. I may have done business with him some time prior to the move."

"Would you mind coming down to the morgue and have a look at the chap? See if you can tell me who he is."

Jonathan paled slightly and Hodgins grinned.

"Don't worry, big brother. He's not been all bashed about. Looks like he's sleeping. Won't take but a minute."

Jonathan got up and walked to the sideboard and poured a whisky, which he downed in one gulp.

"I'd forgotten how squeamish you are. Just like Barnes."

"Yes, you mentioned the lad in your last letter. You weren't all the impressed with him, as I recall.

"He's changed a lot over the year. Going to be a good detective one day. Nice lad. Been courting the young lady next door. Expect they'll be married soon."

"Sounds like you're fond of him. Have I been replaced?"

"Replaced?" Hodgins looked at his brother, surprised by the question.

"We've been apart for a long time. Our correspondence infrequent."

Hodgins thought a moment before speaking. "Yes, I have come to think of him as a brother, but not a replacement. We'll have to make an effort to keep in touch, though."

"You must find time to visit us in Boston. We can go fishing like we used to."

"Haven't gone fishing in years. I believe I still have

our old poles up in the attic."

"Too cold to use them now, but I'm sure there's something else we can find to do. Maybe included that Barnes chap.

CHAPTER FOUR

G rey clouds blocked the sun making the morning eerily dank. Hodgins sensed the dread in his brother grow as they approached the city morgue. Jonathan stood at the foot of the stairs, his complexion pale despite the redness from the cold. Hodgins placed a hand on Jonathan's shoulder.

"Are you ready? Will only take a minute. I promise. Just try to think of him as though he's sleeping, like I mentioned yesterday.

Jonathan nodded and they entered the morgue, gagging as the rotting stench of the corpse hit his nose.

"Guess it is rather ripe in here," Hodgins said. "Good thing you didn't have breakfast. I'd say you'll get used to it, but you won't. Try not to think about it. Works for me. Quick look and we'll be on our way."

Hodgins motioned for the coroner to expose the victim. Dr. McKenzie lifted the white sheet that shrouded the corpse.

"Dear God!"

"You know him?" Hodgins asked.

Jonathan gagged again. "His face. It's swollen, but I recognize him. Brown. Anthony Brown. Worthless piece of trash."

"Not a friend then?" Hodgins grinned. "Your colour's coming back. Wasn't all that bad now, was it?" He turned to McKenzie. "May as well cover him back up."

Jonathan turned and hurried back out into the cold. When Hodgins joined him, Jonathan was leaning against the stone wall, eyes closed, breathing deeply. He jumped when his brother touched him.

"I didn't realize you'd be so shaken up. I'm sorry, but it was necessary."

Jonathan nodded. "I understand. It was the smell more than the dead body."

"Try going in there on a hot summer day." Hodgins' smile disappeared as Jonathan gagged and ran to the side of the steps. "Just like Barnes," he mumbled.

Jonathan pulled out a hanky and wiped his mouth, "Barnes? That constable of yours? What about him?"

Hodgins chuckled. "Reacts the same way. I need to get a statement from you, but what's say we have a drink, to steady the nerves?"

"Good idea."

They walked in silence for several blocks before

Hodgins hailed a passing hansom. "Yonge and Queen," he told the driver.

Hodgins tried talking to Jonathan, but he was still too disturbed by his visit to the morgue. Jonathan leaned against the side of the cab, eyes closed, so Hodgins settled back, listening to the soft clomp of the hooves as the horse made its way to their destination. He gently shook Jonathan when they arrived.

Hodgins paid the driver while Jonathan took in the surroundings. "The Bay Horse Hotel. It's still here? We spent a lot of our time here before the accident." Jonathan turned to his brother "I'd like to visit their graves before I go back to Boston."

"I'll ask Delia to help the children make a special wreath and we can all visit Mama and Papa's graves before Christmas. Now, let's get inside and find a spot near the fire."

The hotel had both a dining room and a lounge with a bar. They chose to sit in the lounge and found an empty table close to the brick fireplace. It was too early for lunch so they had the room almost to themselves.

The open shutters on the windows allowed sunlight to fill the room, making it seem somewhat cheery, despite the lack of decorations. The only staff was a familiar-looking barman, who came over as soon as they were seated.

"Jonathan Hodgins. Ain't seen you in here for…" He shrugged as he tried to remember.

"Over a decade," Jonathan said. "Can't say I've missed seeing your ugly mug."

The barman slapped him on the back, laughing. "You still chasing the ladies?"

"No. I'm married, with two wonderful children. Have a thriving business down in Boston."

"Jonathan came up for Christmas. His family will be joining us Friday. We just came in for a quiet chat and to get reacquainted. What better place then the Bay Horse?" Hodgins said.

"Well, I'll leave you to it then. What'll it be? First drink's on the house."

"I'll have a beer, and I think Jonathan could use a whisky."

"Make it a double."

Their drinks were in front of them minutes later. Jonathan downed his whisky while Hodgins twirled a glass of beer. "Tell me about Brown. You said he was a piece of trash. What did he do? How do you know him?"

"Used to work for me. When I started to relocate my shipping business closer to the docks I discovered he'd been stealing from me. I admit I hadn't checked him out before hiring him as I needed the help and he was strong and available. I was more interested in his muscles than his character. As my business grew, I needed more help and he recommended a couple of blokes."

Jonathan stopped and indicated for the barman to bring another shot.

"My bookkeeping skills aren't very good. You remember when I tried to help Father with the books at the store? Got a right ear-full and sent back to stocking the shelves. I didn't need help with the accounts at first, as I was just starting. Nothing complicated. As I gradually became established over the years I began making good money so I didn't care about how up-to-date anything was, both the accounts and the inventory. Elizabeth insisted I put everything in order before the move. Found out the bugger'd been stealing from me for years, along with his two friends. Fired all three on the spot."

The whisky came and disappeared as fast as the first. "God, will anything get rid of the taste that smell left in my mouth?"

"Slow down, Jonathan. I don't want to have to carry you home before lunchtime. And that taste will go away. So, you fired them. That's all?"

Jonathan couldn't look his brother in the eye. He slid the glass across the table, from hand to hand, staring at the tabletop.

"No." He stopped sliding the glass and rubbed his left arm. Jonathan's voice dropped to little more than a whisper. "I started asking around, telling some business acquaintances about them. Warning them. Word spread and Brown and his friends couldn't get work. They came after me, Bertie."

Hodgins sipped his beer, waiting, remembering when their father tried to pry anything out of Jonathan. Patience was something Albert hadn't inherited and he hoped it wouldn't take all day. By the time Hodgins finished his beer, Jonathan resumed his tale.

"The three of them jumped me one night after I closed up. Fortunately, a few of the dock workers were nearby and came to my aid. Always knew it would come in handy one day to stay on friendly terms with the men on the docks. They knocked all three unconscious. They were still out when I limped back with the police."

"Why didn't you tell me about that? Is that why you stopped writing me? Were you injured? Three against one. You've never been much of a fighter."

"Broken nose, fractured arm, and more bruises than I could count." Jonathan smiled. "I suppose it's high-time I learned to fight, now that I'm closer to the docks. Lot more men like Brown hanging around down there. Can't expect to find a friendly dock worker handy all the time."

"That's the smartest thing I've heard you say all morning. One of my men is a champion boxer. Champion among all the station houses that is. How about I ask him to give you a few lessons?

"Appreciate that, little brother."

Since there seemed to be nothing left to say and it was close to noon, Hodgins waved over the barman and ordered two steak and kidney pies and a pot of tea.

"I think we can forego a formal statement," Hodgins said. "I'll just add a few lines to the file. If we need any additional information, I can write it up at home."

When they finished lunch, Jonathan decided he felt well enough to do some Christmas shopping while Hodgins went to the station.

* * *

Hodgins walked over to Barnes' desk and handed him a piece of paper. "Here, put this in the file. Dead man's got a name now. Anthony Brown." He looked around. "Where's Baxter? Did he finish that sketch of Brown? I'd like to take I with me. Where's the train schedule? Time to go to Aurora and visit the ropemaker. Campbell, I believe? See what he has to say about the envelope containing that fifty dollars."

Barnes pulled a well-used schedule out of his desk

drawer. It'd been folded in haste multiple times and was full of creases, rips and even had a corner missing. Barnes smoothed it out best he could and turned it to face Hodgins.

After studying it for a minute, Hodgins placed his index finger part way down one of the columns. "Here. First train out tomorrow isn't too early. I can be at the Aurora depot shortly after ten." He peered up at Barnes. "Don't suppose we have a map of Aurora?"

Barnes shrugged. "Don't recall ever having need of one, but I'll check. We have maps of most of the towns. Have you ever been up there?"

"Never had the need. One of these days I'll have to plan some trips around the area with the family. Remember the trips we had to make to Stouffville last January? Your first murder investigation. Pretty little village. Maybe in the spring we can pick a spot and hop on the train. Wonder if they allow dogs on the train?"

"Sounds like quite an adventure."

"Maybe if you're still courting that pretty little neighbour of mine, you can both join us."

Barnes turned pink and stammered. "Well… maybe… you see…"

"Trouble?"

"No, sir." Barnes looked around and noticed several

of the constables listening and snickering.

Hodgins asked him to step into his office, closing the door behind them.

"What's wrong lad?"

Barnes looked at the floor and shuffled his feet.

"You know I'll help any way I can, but you need to tell me what's wrong."

Barnes mumbled, head still down.

"Speak up, Constable. And look at me. Please."

Barnes raised his head and looked directly at Hodgins and a lopsided grin slowly appeared on his face. "I was going to ask her to marry me."

Hodgins came around the desk and slapped Barnes on the back. "Congratulations, Henry. She's a lovely girl, and her folks seem quite taken with you."

"And my Ma likes her, and my little sister gets along with her like they're old friends. I was thinking of asking her after Christmas. Maybe New Year's Eve."

"That's wonderful news. I'm sure my wife will want to throw you a party."

Barnes' eyes went wide. "What if she says no? You can't tell anyone. Not even Mrs. Hodgins."

"You're secret's safe with me. Now why don't you send a wire to the Boston Police Department and see what they can tell us about Brown. I'll see if I can find anyone who saw the two tramps. They may have jumped on one of the trains."

Barnes went to send the telegraph and Hodgins bundled up in his overcoat and scarf and started out to Union Station. The biting wind had died off and it was turning into a nice day, so he decided to walk. It gave him time to think. So many changes were coming. Eighteen hundred and seventy five was going to be different. Hodgins couldn't believe Dr. McKenzie was handing in his resignation and moving back to Inverness. What type of person would be replacing him? Would the new coroner get along with him and the rest of the police? Barnes would likely be getting married in the spring. Hodgins had no doubt she'd say yes. He'd seen the couple together many times. They were mad about each other. Over the past year he had taken Barnes under his wing, grooming him to one day be a detective. They'd grown close; Barnes, a substitute for the brother that had moved out of the country a decade ago; and Hodgins, a replacement for the father Barnes had recently lost. Before he knew it, Hodgins had made it to Simcoe Street and Union Station.

He bypassed the main building and headed for the tracks. If the tramps had jumped the train, they wouldn't have been seen by the employees inside. Hodgins noticed the station agent had wrangled one of the railway constables into helping clear the snow off the platform. They'd moved down to the tracks to clear the plank walkways used by employees by the time Hodgins reached them. He identified himself and gave a description of the tramps.

"Have you seen them around here lately? Or maybe someone reported seeing them hanging about?"

"Yes," the constable said. "I recall them. Don't see too many white men travelling with a negro. Chased them off the train yesterday. Can't say for certain they didn't come back."

Hodgins wandered the surrounding area questioning the men working for the shipping companies loading freight cars, preparing them for hook-up and departure. No one actually saw the tramps leave the area so it was possible they'd doubled back, jumped onto a car farther along the tracks, and were long gone. He checked back with the station agent to see where the trains were headed around the time the tramps were seen, and had telegraphs sent to all the possible stops. If they got off somewhere they would've been seen.

Not anxious to make the trek back to the station, he lingered near the wood stove in the waiting area. Even if he took the trolley, he'd still have some walking to do. Frustration at not being able to track down the tramps built up and he swore. No one was waiting for a train, so he wasn't concerned about keeping his voice down. After circling the stove a few times, he made his way over to the station agent.

"Do you think it at all possible those two tramps hopped the train without being seen?"

The station master shrugged. "Anything's possible, Detective. Not enough employees to watch every inch of the track."

"Yes, I know about not having enough men. In your opinion, where's the most likely spot they could've managed it?"

"Oh, that's easy. Westbound, just past where Queen and King meet and the tracks bend off. Eastbound, maybe around the dry dock or anywhere north of Kingston Road. Only things east of De Grassi are farm lands. No one to see what you're up to 'cepting a bunch of cows."

Hodgins smiled. "Somehow I don't think I'd get much out of them, except maybe a bucket of milk." He extended his hand. "Thank you for all your assistance. I'll have one of my constables check in with you to see if anyone answers the telegrams."

Hodgins raised his collar and fastened the top button before heading out to catch a trolley. The wind had picked up while at Union Station and he didn't relish the forty-minute walk back to the station on Wilton Avenue.

He arrived to find Barnes at his desk, a map folded out across it. "Found a map of Aurora. It's not very big. The town that is. Couldn't find a business directory."

"I'll ask around when I arrive. Town that size, probably won't be difficult to find someone who knows where I can find the ropemaker."

CHAPTER FIVE

Next morning Hodgins sat on the train headed north. Settling back, he opened the morning issue of the Globe and Mail, hoping the two-hour ride would pass quickly. He'd ridden enough trains to barely notice the constant rocking. The train slowed once shortly after leaving the station and he asked a porter what the problem was.

"Nothing to worry 'bout Mister. Lots of snow on the tracks. Jest taking it easy-like."

He nodded and the porter moved on to answer questions from other passengers and check tickets. Hodgins listened briefly to some of the conversations around him. Most were discussions of Christmas events, family gatherings, and gifts. It seemed quite a number of people would be receiving hand-knit sweaters, mittens, and scarves.

Trying to ignore the voices, he skimmed the front page, chuckling at the advertisement for Christmas Cattle. An image of cows wearing garlands, with a little silver star on their heads, passed through his mind. Farther in was another ad, this one more interesting. Comedian John Murray was appearing at the Royal Opera House in Rip Van Winkle. He tore it out and stuffed it in his pocket, thinking it might be a pleasant outing once Jonathan's family arrived.

Hodgins turned back to the news. Constable McClennan from Station One arrested two people for assaulting a street car driver. He clicked his tongue in disbelief at people's horrid behaviour. The city had become crime-ridden lately. Men being assaulted simply for doing their jobs, and more than the usual amount of shoplifting. He thought about the items he'd heard about. Small things: silver bracelets, lace handkerchiefs, even socks. The one person who'd been caught said it was a Christmas gift for his wife. Times were hard and people did what they had to. Unfortunately, more than one family would have someone in jail for the holidays.

As he started his third time through the paper, the train finally pulled into the station in Aurora. Once it came to a stop, Hodgins assisted a young mother off, taking her parcels so she could carry the baby. After handing the packages off to her waiting husband, Hodgins asked him if he knew where Campbell's was. The young man directed him to the ropemaker's place of business on Yonge Street.

Hodgins hadn't realized Yonge went so far north. He pictured the map of the rail line that ran this way and wondered if the road continued all the way up as well. As he stood at the corner of Yonge and Wellington he looked north at the long stretch of road. Campbell's business was just a short walk away. A long building, about fourteen feet wide, sat on the west side of Yonge, just north of Wellington. Hodgins guessed the building had to be several hundred feet long. He walked through the main door and saw only a few men working inside. A staircase led up to a door on the second floor, the word *Office* painted in black on the frosted glass. One of the workmen hollered at Hodgins without stopping his work.

"Help you, Mister?"

Hodgins pointed to the office. "Campbell in there?"

"Believe so."

Hodgins made his way to the stairs, weaving through piles of ropes. When he reached the door, he knocked and went in before Campbell could reply. He introduced himself and got straight to the point of his visit.

"Is this one of yours?"

Mr. Campbell took the envelope in his pudgy fingers. "Yes, I suppose so. It looks like my clerk's writing. Why are the police interested in it?

"It was found in the possession of a murder victim.

Just trying to track his whereabouts before he was killed."

"This was found on a dead man you say?"

"Man by the name of Anthony Brown. Do you know him?

Campbell shook his head. "Name doesn't sound familiar, but then again, I do business with folks from out of town and don't know them all by name. Not every one asks for paperwork."

"He's about five foot six, late thirties, black hair, bushy beard." Hodgins pulled a piece of paper from his jacket and unfolded it. "One of my men sketched him. Does he look familiar? It's a pretty good likeness."

Campbell studied the sketch for a moment. "Sorry, I can't help."

"Well then, can you tell me why he'd have one of your envelopes, containing fifty dollars?"

Campbell's attitude changed. He stood straight, pulling his shoulders back and his eyes narrowed, making them all but disappear among the folds of fat. "What are you implying, Detective? Why, anyone could have found that envelope and used it for their own purpose. Fifty dollars! That's quite a sum. You aren't suggesting something underhanded?"

"No, not at all. As you say, the envelope could have come from anyone. Somebody may have taken one from your office, or even removed it from the trash bin."

Suspicion deflected, Campbell relaxed a little, but remained guarded. "Don't keep the office door locked. People go in and out all the time."

"Would you mind if I spoke to your employees? Show them the sketch?"

"Certainly. Always willing to cooperate with the constabulary. Don't think you'll find any of them can help. Trust my employees completely."

Campbell escorted Hodgins through the factory down a walkway that ran the length of the building along the south wall. The main work area sat a few feet lower. Several strands of rope of varying lengths stretched from one end to the other, supported by trestles every ten feet or so.

A foreman paced along the walkway, watching the process and barking out orders. They stopped to show him the picture of Brown. He didn't recognize him, and handed the sketch back to Hodgins before resuming his yelling.

"Why are there men running back and forth?" Hodgins asked Campbell.

"They're guiding the rope, making sure it twists properly. Call them donkeys. The fibres are short, so they need to be twisted together properly or they won't hold.

As the rope twists it gets shorter. The drive mechanism at that end moves as the rope length changes." Campbell pointed at the other end. "Those ends are fixed in place. Once the rope is done, it's wound onto those wooden reels, over on the north side."

"Looks simple enough," Hodgins said.

"Like to give it a go?" Campbell asked.

Hodgins smiled. "Don't suppose I'll ever get another opportunity. Never know when a new skill could come in handy."

"Follow me. Making some rope for a freight ship at the far end." He led Hodgins to another set-up, much larger than the last. Instead of thin strands attached to several hooks, strands already twisted together forming ropes about two inches thick were being worked into one larger rope, with the aid of an exceptionally large crank.

"Wally, give this detective a go, will you?"

Hodgins grasped the crank and started to turn. "My word! It's harder than it looks." He grabbed the handle with both hands and turned it again. Exhausted after only a few turns, he relinquished the crank to Wally. "I think I'll stick to police work." He reached into his pocket and pulled out the sketch of Brown. "Ever seen this guy?"

When Wally took the sketch, his rough and calloused hands practically crushed the paper. Hodgins looked down at his own hands, surprised to see a redness to them after only turning the crank a few times.

"Sure, I know 'im. Why that's Tony. Can't say where's I've seen him for a bit. His wife probably knows where he's got to."

Hodgins raised an eyebrow at the familiar use of the nickname Tony and wondered why Jonathan hadn't mentioned Brown was married. "Don't suppose you'll be seeing him again. He was murdered Friday evening. You say he has a wife? Where might I find her?"

Wally dropped the sketch. "Murdered?" He took a step back. "You don't think I did it, do you? Ain't see him for ages."

"No, just trying to find out more about him. Who he's seen. Do you know where he lives?"

"Over on Seal Street, other side of the tracks. Number four."

Hodgins picked up the crumpled sketch, thanked the man, then went in search of Mrs. Brown. He never liked having to be the one to tell someone their loved one was dead. Every time he had to, he imagined how Cordelia would react if another officer came to his house to tell her he'd been killed. Twice this year he'd ended up in the hospital and Delia fussed so much he went back to work early. Hard as he tried, he'd never been able to find a nice way to break the news. Probably was no nice way. He ran the words through his mind repeatedly, until he found himself in front of number four.

A chill worked its way through his clothing and into his bones as he stood staring at the tiny house. A gust of wind spurred him up the walk to the door. He hesitated before knocking. After straightening his collar and brushing off some of the snow, he raised his hand. Flakes of faded green paint sprinkled to the porch each time his knuckles hit the door. A young woman wearing a torn apron, loose hairs sticking out of a once tight bun, opened the door. The bulge under her apron told Hodgins she was with child. This was going to be worse than expected. Loud wailing came from somewhere at the back of the house.

"I'm coming," she yelled over her shoulder. She turned back to Hodgins. "It's not a good time. Whatever you're selling, I'm not interested."

"I'm Detective Hodgins, Toronto Constabulary. I need to speak with you."

She glanced at the badge as he pulled back the label of his overcoat. Her shoulders dropped. "Come in." She pointed to a small room on his left.

"The twins just won't stop crying. Please, warm yourself by the fire while I try to quiet the babies."

Hodgins stomped the snow off his boots and finished unbuttoning his topcoat before going to the crackling fire. It wasn't large, but definitely welcome. His stomach rumbled when he caught a whiff of freshly baked bread. Trying to ignore it, he set his thoughts on how to tell Mrs. Brown her husband had been killed.

She wasn't at all what he'd expected based on Jonathan's description of Brown. He expected her to be stocky, like her husband, rather rough, and definitely older. Tired as she was, it wasn't at all difficult to tell she was an extremely handsome young woman. Could it be possible she didn't know what her husband was like? So many men kept their wives in the dark when it came to business dealings, not wanting to muddle their weak minds. Weak indeed. Cordelia was as intelligent as most men he knew, more even. He'd learned early in their marriage just how good a business women she would have been, given the chance. After all, who was it who ran the household and kept most of the household accounts? The wife. The so-called weak woman. He turned at the sound of rustling skirts.

Mrs. Brown joined him in the small sitting room, a sleeping baby in each arm. He estimated they weren't much more than a year old.

"Let me help you." Hodgins took one of the babies

so she could lower herself onto the settee with a semblance of grace.

"I can tell you've a way with babies, Detective… Sorry, what was your name again?

"Detective Hodgins, and yes, I have a daughter, almost grown now. Going on ten." He reached into his pocket and handed her the wrinkled sketch, then sat in a chair opposite her.

She placed the sleeping baby beside her and unfolded the paper. "Why, this is a drawing of my husband." She closed her eyes and took two slow breaths. "What's he done now?"

"Do you have family or friends who can stay with you, or you with them?"

"Please, Detective. I know my Tony isn't a saint. Just tell me what's he done."

"Well, he hasn't actually done anything that I'm aware of. I'm very sorry to tell you, but your husband has been murdered."

Mrs. Brown looked at him as though she didn't understand, cocking her head to one side, then the other. Something in her eyes changed. She seemed to age at least ten years. "D-d-dead? Wait, you said murdered. It wasn't an accident? You're certain of that?"

"Yes, ma'am. Of that I have no doubt. Is there

someone who can stay with you?" He glanced down at her belly as she put her hand on the large bump. "Soon?"

She nodded. "About two months." She picked up the baby and held it close. "Murdered," she mumbled. "But who?"

She looked at him, waiting for an answer. Her eyes grew red and moist, but no tears fell. Mrs. Brown remained remarkably composed. Hodgins wondered if she wasn't all that upset at the news, or simply refused to cry in front of a stranger.

"We don't know, but we're looking into several possibilities."

"Hodgins. I've heard that name before, not recently."

"My brother, Jonathan, knew your husband in Boston."

Her eyes narrowed slightly, her tone changed. "Yes, I recall now." The ice in her voice could have frozen the fire. "If there's nothing else, I have things to attend to. Where is his body? I'd like to send for it."

What else had Jonathan not told him? The look in her eyes now reflected pure hatred. Hodgins felt embarrassed and guilty, even though none of it was his fault. "We'll have him sent up. You won't have to do anything. I'll make the arrangements personally when I return. Shall I have him sent here, or is there another place you'd prefer?"

"Here is just fine, thank you." Her tone now clipped, he knew he'd outstayed his welcome.

"Day after tomorrow, then?"

She nodded, took the baby from him and escorted him to the door. It was too cold to wander around and check out the town, so he went to the Beresford's Railway Hotel on Mosley Street for a bite and beverage while waiting for the train back to Toronto. He showed the sketch to the staff, discovering that Brown had been in a few times, but no one had been on friendly terms with him.

CHAPTER SIX

The train ride back felt longer than the ride up. Hodgins chatted to a fellow passenger about the day's news and half-listened as the gentleman prattled on about his business. Hodgins wasn't particularly interested in learning all about the Provincial Insurance Company, but that didn't deter the man. The train finally arrived in Toronto and Hodgins hurried back to the police station. He almost walked into Barnes as the constable exited the station house.

"Evening, sir. Was your trip a success?" Barnes stood aside to allow Hodgins to get in from the cold.

"If by success you mean do I know who the killer is, then I'm afraid the answer is no." He shook off his coat and draped it over a chair by the wood stove. "Found Brown's widow."

"Breaking the news of a death is the worst part of being a copper."

"You're right about that. Young woman with two small babies, twins, and another on the way. I hope she has family to help her now. Funny, her tone changed when I mentioned her husband knew my brother in Boston. Soon as she heard his name she became almost hostile. All but asked me to leave. Which reminds me, I need to let McKenzie know to ship the body to her. I think I'll head back on Saturday, if I can. I'd like to talk to more people, find out what Anthony Brown was like, and if anyone had any problems with him. So far, I've only got my brother's opinion of him. Brown spent time in jail, so he's no saint, and even his wife first thought I'd come because of trouble. I'd like to hear a few other opinions.

"Surely, you don't doubt your brother's word?"

"No, not at all. But people do tend to exaggerate somewhat. Done it myself on occasion. We need to treat this like any other investigation. Forget he's family and check his story is all I'm saying."

He wondered why Jonathan needed to come up a full week before his family. He'd barely mentioned the business meeting since he'd arrived. As far as Hodgins knew, Jonathan only had that one meeting scheduled. The more he thought about it, the more confused he became. Just when was Jonathan's meeting? There'd been no mention of it, and he never left the house on his own. Any time Jonathan ventured out alone, Scraps had been with him. Not too professional to take a dog to a business meeting. Had he lied about it? Hodgins shook the thoughts from his mind. "Any word from the Boston police on Brown?"

"No, nothing yet. I'm sure we'll hear soon."

"If there's no word in a few days, ask again. Now off home with you. I've held you up long enough."

Hodgins went into his office and spent the next half hour writing up his notes and adding his thoughts before going home, too.

* * *

Dinner was quieter than usual. Both brothers avoided talking of the deceased and anything related to the case, but the looks they exchanged gave away their thoughts. Hodgins wondered if there could be the slightest possibility Jonathan was involved in the death of Brown. Could Jonathan have changed so much over the past ten years? He dealt with a lot of rough people, and Hodgins' suspected not all of Jonathan's customers even remotely resembled upstanding citizens. Cordelia finally broke the silence.

"I'm so looking forward to seeing Elizabeth again, and finally meeting your children. We keep saying we're going to go down for a visit, but it just never happens."

"Oh, yes," Sara chimed in. "I've got so many things to show them. And we can make Christmas decorations."

"Their train will be here Friday afternoon. Elizabeth spoke of little else right up to my boarding. She hollered something as the train pulled out, but the hiss of steam drowned her out," Jonathan said. "And Cora's looking forward to meeting her cousin. Little Freddie's more excited about the train ride."

Hodgins pushed the case to the back of his mind and joined in. "Likes trains, does he? Well, I have a little pull around here. I'm certain I can arrange a tour of Union Station. Maybe even a short ride with the engineer. Think he'll enjoy that?"

"I'm sure he will. So will I, truth be told. Remember that train Father gave me for Christmas when I was six?"

"Don't tell me you still have it? Last time I saw it, most of the paint had peeled off."

"It's the only thing I have to remind me of him. Must have taken him days to carve it. The wheels still turn. Keep it on the top shelf of the bookcase in my office."

They chatted about the arrangements for Jonathan's family, then Sara helped clear up and wash dishes. Jonathan settled in front of the fire with a book while Hodgins took Scraps for a walk.

With the evening reasonably mild, the air crisp, wandering around the neighbourhood with the dog relaxed him. It gave him time to mull over the facts of the case. He wished he could find the time alone with Delia to go over this with her. Hodgins' and Scraps walked up and down several streets, enjoying the solitude. Few buggies were about and he only encountered one other person out for a constitutional. He recognized the man but couldn't recall his name.

As he approached home, he noticed Barnes entering the house next door, and smiled. Cordelia would be furious that Hodgins hadn't told her about Barnes intention to propose to their beautiful, young neighbour, but he'd promised the lad he'd keep his secret.

CHAPTER SEVEN

Hodgins woke several times during the night, pondering how much his brother had changed. He longed to go over everything with Delia as she had a way of making him pull the facts together. She looked so peaceful, not restless like him. Hodgins sat on the edge of the bed and cleared his throat. Delia murmured and rolled over. He rose and walked to her side of the bed, reaching down to gently shake her shoulder. He stopped inches away. The next few weeks would be hectic. He didn't have the heart to disturb her knowing how little sleep awaited her. Sighing, he crawled back into bed, his childhood memories of Jonathan pushing their way to the front of his mind.

They'd been close growing up and remained so even into adulthood, or so he'd thought. Why hadn't Jonathan told him about the attack by his former employees? Was there something he wasn't saying about Mrs. Brown? There was no mistaking the change in her demeanor and attitude once she realized he was Jonathan's brother. Had

Jonathan fallen in with a bad lot in Boston? Was it even slightly possible he'd murdered someone? How could he possibly arrest his own brother, and at Christmas-time? If found guilty, he'd hang.

Hodgins stared at the ceiling, watching the shadows shift as the wind raced through the branches, rearranging them and pushing the clouds along. Unable to fall back asleep, he rose, went down to the sitting room and lit the fire. The tall clock in the hall showed 3:05. Scraps padded in and lay on the rag-rug in front of the fire, completely unconcerned as to why someone was up so early. Hodgins sat staring at the writing on the pages of his notebook. Nothing came together. He tapped his pencil on the book, and Scraps raised his head and barked softly, tail thumping on the floor. Hodgins leaned forward and scratched the dog's head.

"Maybe a walk, eh boy?"

Scraps sat up, tail thumping faster. Hodgins went over to the window to check the weather. It wasn't snowing and the wind had died down somewhat.

"You're in luck boy. Seems like a fine night for a quick stroll."

Hodgins slipped the notebook into the drawer of the side table before heading upstairs to dress. When he came down, Scraps sat at the door, leash in mouth. He'd quickly learned by putting his big, hairy paws on the wall, he was tall enough to remove the leash from the hook. Hodgins put on his overcoat and leather gloves, then wound a scarf around his neck before removing the leash from Scrap's mouth and fastening it to the collar. With Scraps pulling him along, they ventured out into the darkness.

Hodgins found the stillness comforting. The silence of the early morning broke only with the occasional clump of snow falling from a branch or rooftop. The air was colder than expected, making both his and Scraps' breath visible. Hodgins cursed himself for not bringing a lantern. Clouds filled the already blackened sky, blocking what little light there was. They strolled along the road, not needing to be concerned about dodging horses, sleighs, or buggies. Scraps trotted ahead, tail up, enjoying the unexpected romp. Hodgins followed behind mindlessly, paying no attention to where the dog led him.

Usually, quiet walks helped sort out his thoughts, but it wasn't working. When they approached the next street, Hodgins looked up at the street sign, surprised to find they'd crossed Yonge Street and were already up at Mount Pleasant and St. Clair. It was after four-thirty when they returned home. He fed Scraps and headed back to bed, hoping to get a couple hours sleep.

* * *

The aroma of coffee roused Hodgins from a deep sleep. Muffled voices mixed with the sizzle of the sausages caught his attention. They had company. He dressed, glancing at his pocket watch before placing it in his jacket pocket. It was almost nine thirty—way past his time. He raced down the stairs and into the kitchen. Barnes sat at the table with Cordelia and Jonathan, enjoying breakfast.

"Why didn't you wake me?

"You had such a restless night I didn't think a few extra hours would hurt." Cordelia placed a plate in front of him, and kissed his cheek. "Did you have a nice walk this morning?"

Hodgins raised an eyebrow. "I didn't realize you were awake. It was all for naught, anyway. I just can't figure this one out." He looked over at Barnes. "Inspector angry?"

"No, sir." Barnes swallowed the last bite of his sausage. "He hasn't come in yet either. Finally received a reply from Boston, though. Thought you'd want to know." His eyes flicked towards Jonathan briefly. "Some interesting information."

"You can tell me all about it on the way in." Hodgins scarfed down his breakfast and hurried Barnes out the door.

"May as well take a cab. There's a small coupe there, on the corner." The men hurried along the road, calling out for him to wait.

"Station House Four," Hodgins told the driver. Once seated, the detective rapped on the roof and the driver snapped his reins, jerking the coupe when the horses suddenly moved. Their hooves barely made a sound, the packed snow muffling their steps.

They settled back, blanket over their laps. "I assume there's something about my brother in the report from the Boston police? Something unpleasant?"

"Yes, sir." Barnes looked down, twisting the edge of the wool blanket.

"Out with it, lad. Forget he's my brother."

"It's nothing major, just a few drunken brawls. And one complaint from a lady."

Hodgins turned to face Barnes. "A lady? What type of complaint?"

"Lewd comments, unwanted attention, if you catch my drift."

Hodgins was shocked. Could his brother have been unfaithful? He'd have to have a long talk with him before his family arrived on the weekend.

"Who made the complaint?" Hodgins hoped it wasn't who he suspected.

"Mrs. Brown."

"Damn. Our Mr. Brown's wife? Well, she is quite

attractive, and young. I'm beginning to think I don't know my brother as well as I thought. I hope it went no further."

Hodgins glanced out the tiny window, spotting a boy on the corner waving the morning edition at passers-by. He hoped it contained nothing about Brown's murder and the lack of information the police had. "What about Mr. Brown? Anything on him?"

"His last release was in July. Seems he was in and out of jail on a regular basis. They didn't know he'd left town. Got quite a lengthy record, going back to when he was a lad. Apparently, he's been out on the streets since he was six or seven. Stealing at first, then assault and extortion. Put more than one bloke in the hospital. Sounds like no one will miss him, except maybe his wife. She's been arrested a few times, too. Mainly petty theft. Nothing recent."

"I'm not completely certain his wife will miss him," Hodgins mumbled, more to himself than to Barnes.

As soon as they arrived at the station house, Hodgins paid the cab driver while Barnes went ahead to retrieve the report from his desk. He joined Hodgins in his office.

"Any word on those two tramps? They must be somewhere. Can't have vanished into thin air."

"Nothing yet. I'm planning on going down to Union to chat with the station agent. See if they've any word from the other train stations."

"Off with you then. We need find those two."

* * *

An hour later Barnes returned. He raced into Hodgins' office, a huge grin plastered across his face. "Telegram came into Union Station while I was there." Barnes handed the paper to Hodgins before brushing the snow from his shoulders. "They've been spotted west of here, over in Berlin. Two tramps were thrown off the train just before it pulled out last night. One white man, one coloured. Must be the same ones. Might still be there."

"Good. I believe Berlin has a sheriff, so wire him and ask him to round up some men to find the tramps and hold them somewhere. Promise them food and shelter from the cold. Warm feet and a full belly should keep them content until I can arrive."

"Right away, sir."

Hodgins decided to take a break from the case and go through some old files. He still had a couple of unsolved deaths from earlier in the year. Suspicious, but indeterminate if they were murders or accidents. He needed the distraction. Hodgins stood and stretched out his back, then went out to the filing cabinets and rummaged through the drawers, not looking for anything in particular. His fingers stopped when he came to a file labelled *Willson, Unsolved.*

Several hours and many cups of tea later, he hadn't discovered anything new in the Willson shooting. When he returned the file to the cabinet, Hodgins noticed how dark it had become outside. He pulled out his pocket watch. Almost seven. He grabbed his coat, but as he passed Sergeant Evans' desk, the clicking of the telegraph machine stopped him. Hodgins waited while the sergeant wrote up the message and handed it to him. Finally, the reply from Berlin saying they had the two tramps. Hodgins wired back that he'd take the first train out in the morning.

CHAPTER EIGHT

That evening, Hodgins joined Cordelia and Sara in the kitchen, watching while they prepared the evening meal. Sara peeled and cut the potatoes then placed them in a pot of water, struggling to carry it to the wood stove. Hodgins got up to help, but Sara refused.

"I'm old enough to do it by myself." Both hands gripped the handle as she made her way across the kitchen. She managed the trip without spilling any water, but couldn't lift it high enough to set it on the stove.

Hodgins rushed over, relieving her of the load. "Don't want you to burn yourself. And don't ever be afraid to ask for help, no matter how old you get."

Sara pouted and crossed her arms.

"I know you're old enough, you're just not tall enough." He tugged her braid. "Maybe I can build you a step until you grow a little more."

Sara threw back her head and stomped to the sink to chop the carrots. Hodgins followed and reached over to steal one.

"Don't know if I'll return before Jonathan's family arrives on Friday. I hope to take the last train back tomorrow, but I'll plan on staying over for a day or two in case the weather turns."

"Don't rush the investigation," Delia said. "If you have to stay for a few day, I'll simply have Jonathan hire a carriage to pick his family up."

"Can we all go?" Sara pleaded. "Please?"

"I don't see why not," Hodgins said. "Better hire two carriages. Won't be enough room in one for everyone plus their luggage. Their train should be pulling in shortly after two. I'll ask Barnes to check for any delays, and I'll wire him if I'll be late getting back from Berlin. I'll try my best to get home in time. With luck, I'll be escorting two prisoners."

"I'll pack up some leftovers for the train ride. No sense spending good money on stale sandwiches."

"Where's Jonathan? I need to talk to him."

"He took Scraps for a walk."

"No wonder the house is so quiet. It's cold, so I don't imagine they'll be out long." He took out his pocket watch to check the time. "It's already after seven-thirty. They should have the sense to be home by now. When did they leave?"

"Oh, about thirty minutes ago, I guess." Cordelia

covered the pot of boiling potatoes, then added another log to the fire below before joining him at the table. "What's troubling you, Bertie? You've barely mentioned the case. That's not like you at all. Is your brother somehow involved?"

"Never could hide anything from you, Delia. I honestly don't know if he's involved. I do know there's secrets he's keeping. Just don't know if they're relevant. He's not the same man I grew up with. That much I do know for certain."

Before Cordelia could press him for more information, they heard barking from the back yard. The outer door to the small porch slammed and Cordelia hurried to the kitchen door, making sure it couldn't open, trapping the wet dog and Jonathan.

"Sara, rub him down with that old blanket. I don't want mud and snow tracked through my clean house."

Jonathan edged the door open an inch. "I assume you're referring to the dog and not me." He slipped off his overcoat and draped it on the back of a chair, while Sara rubbed down Scraps, giggling at her uncle's remark. He placed his overshoes beside the chair and stepped into the kitchen. "Why the serious face brother?"

"We need to talk." Hodgins walked down the hall and into the sitting room, Jonathan close behind. Hodgins faced the fire, hands clasped behind his back.

"Have I done something to anger you, little brother?"

"Why didn't you tell me what happened in Boston?"

"As I said earlier, I didn't want to worry you. The attack was brief, the men arrested and jailed."

"Not that." Albert turned to face Jonathan. "Why didn't you tell me about Mrs. Brown?"

"Oh." Jonathan dropped onto the closest chair and buried his face in his hands. "It's not something I'm proud of. I was drunk." He looked up, hands raised. "I know. That doesn't excuse my behaviour. Lizzie was away with the children, visiting her parents. We needed a break from each other. How could I possibly tell my younger brother that my marriage was a failure? I'm the eldest and should be setting an example. And you've always had such high morals. Everything was always right or wrong, nothing in between. I was drunk and missing my wife. Janel came in, looking for her husband. I tried to take advantage."

"Janel?" You're on familiar terms with her? How far did it go?"

Jonathan got up and stood beside Albert, placing his hand on his arm. "You have to believe me, Albert. Nothing happened. One of Brown's cohorts was in the bar and escorted Janel, Mrs. Brown, home, then told Tony.

Albert brushed Jonathan's hand away. "I've seen the

report from Boston. It happened shortly before your attack. Could it be he was less concerned with being fired and more concerned about his wife's honour?"

Jonathan shrugged. "Maybe a little of both."

"Does Elizabeth know?"

"Dear God, no. As soon as my bruises and broken arm healed I went to her parents' home and pleaded with her to return with me. Promised I'd spend less time at work and more time with my family. We're quite content now. Won't ever have what you have with Cordelia, but we're happy enough."

Albert tried to read Jonathan's expression while listening to the sorrow in his voice. *He's my brother. I have to believe him.*

"Then we won't speak of it again. Please, no more secrets. Drink before we eat?"

Sara burst into the room, half-dried dog at her side. "Mommy said supper's ready."

She grabbed her father's hand and practically dragged him down the hall and into the kitchen. Once they were seated and served, Sara did most of the talking while they ate, listing everything she planned on doing with her cousins. The list didn't change much from one meal to another, but she seemed to be including more decorations. Hodgins wondered where they'd find space for them all.

"I've waited ever so long to meet Cora." Sara rattled on, pausing occasionally to eat. "We write all the time. I've even made her a Christmas gift, but it's a secret."

Hodgins nodded and smiled, only half listening as he thought about his conversation with Jonathan. Sara would be meeting her two cousins for the first time and he was beginning to feel like he was meeting his brother for the first time as well.

Once the meal was over, dishes washed and put away, Sara got ready for bed. The two brothers headed to the sitting room; Jonathan chose to read, while Albert decided to get some sleep.

"I have an early train to catch, so I'll bid you goodnight. Keep an eye on everyone while I'm gone. Not certain when I'll be back. It all depends on how it goes with the two tramps. I'll wire if I'm delayed past Friday."

Jonathan glanced up from his book. "Don't worry about us. We'll be fine. I hope you find your murderer. Not that I'm sorry Brown's dead."

"Don't suppose you're alone with that sentiment," Hodgins remarked before heading upstairs. He was about to climb into bed when Cordelia came into the bedroom.

"There's a piece of beef and a couple of biscuits wrapped in a cloth in the tin by the window. Don't want the mice to get it before you do. Is everything sorted with

Jonathan?"

"Yes. Seems he and Elizabeth had a spot of trouble and separated briefly. He says they're fine now. Don't mention it when she arrives."

"She may want to talk about it, but I'll wait until she brings it up. If she doesn't I'll mention a friend who's having trouble. Maybe it'll encourage her to say something."

Hodgins walked over and kissed her forehead. "I've no doubt you'll find out and make her believe it was all her idea to tell you."

CHAPTER NINE

Hodgins rose before the sun the next morning. The birds hadn't even woke yet. Off in the distance horse bells jingled. "At least I'm not the only fool up this early," he mumbled while packing a few things in a carryall, before attending to his morning routine. After dressing, he started a fire in the fireplace so Cordelia would wake to a warm room, then made his way downstairs, avoiding the one step that always squeaked.

Once in the kitchen, he started a fire in the stove and put the kettle on to boil, then lit the fire in the sitting room. The downstairs would be comfortably warm by the time the household awoke. When he returned to the kitchen, Scraps had moved over by the heat and gone back to sleep. Hodgins retrieved his lunch from the tin, placed it in his carryall, then searched for the rest of the biscuits in the ice chest. He set two of them on the stove to warm while he poured his tea, and managed to grab the biscuits before they blackened, almost dropping them as they burned his fingers. He slathered them in some of

Cordelia's homemade apple jelly and watched as it melted into the crevices. Tea drank and biscuits devoured, he slipped on his overcoat, wrapped his scarf around his neck and headed out the door.

With no cabbies in sight he had to walk several blocks before finding a ride. Despite having his gloved hands buried in his pockets, his fingers were practically frozen by the time he hailed a cab and wrapped himself in the passenger blanket.

When he arrived at Union Station, the platform and waiting lounge were practically empty. The hour was too early for most travellers. The few individuals about were loading freight into wagons, probably brought in by White Star's *Atlantic*, sitting in the harbour since yesterday. Hodgins wondered if that's who Jonathan's meeting was with. A lucrative contact if won. He ambled to an empty bench beside the pot belly stove in the waiting area after purchasing his ticket. Fifteen minutes later, he was seated on the seven-thirty train. It was scheduled to arrive in Berlin at ten-thirty, so he placed his ticket on his lap and immediately fell asleep.

About two hours later he woke to find a young boy sitting across from him, staring. Hodgins smiled at him, but his expression never changed. A woman sat beside the boy, sleeping.

"What's your name?"

Nothing. The child didn't even blink. Hodgins shrugged and checked the time. The train was due at the Berlin station in another hour. He pulled out his notebook to find the Sheriff's name—Davidson. One of the porters walked through the car, so Hodgins asked if he knew where to find Davidson. Hodgins noticed the boys eyes widen when he mentioned the sheriff.

Hodgins continued to read and re-read his notes. He looked up when he noticed the train slow, followed by the shriek of the whistle. Hodgins peered out the window, and the town eventually came into view. He placed his carryall on the empty seat beside him, ready to exit as soon as the train pulled in. The squeal of the breaks finally woke the woman across from him. The boy sat up on his knees and whispered something in her ear. She turned her gaze towards Hodgins. He smiled and introduced himself.

"Good morning ma'am. Couldn't help but notice your boy's interest when I asked about the sheriff. I'm Detective Hodgins from the Toronto Constabulary.

The little boy's mouth dropped open. "A real detective?"

"Yes, a real, honest-to-goodness detective."

"Little Alfy's fascinated with lawmen. He was ever so excited when we took him to see The Scouts of the Prairie last year while we were in Norfolk. We even met Buffalo Bill and Ned Buntline afterwards."

Alfy's head bobbed up and down while his mother spoke. "They kilt real injuns. A whole bunch of 'em," he added.

Hodgins smiled and ruffled the boy's hair. "I'm sure they did. If you'd ever like a tour of a police station next time you're in Toronto, just come to Station Four. Tell them Detective Hodgins invited you. Enjoy your day."

The train finally came to a stop and Hodgins exited. The wind wasn't as strong now and the sun had warmed the air, but he still tightened his scarf as he hurried along the streets, trying to follow the directions given him. He located the sheriff easily. Unlike Hodgins' large brick station house, Berlin's station was a board and batten building. The main office was one room, not more than forty feet square. A bulletin board hung on the wall, half filled with posters, most of which Hodgins recognized. A single file cabinet stood beside it, with a pot belly stove a few feet away. The sheriff's desk was just off to the right of the door, with a rather large man sitting behind it. They chatted briefly before Hodgins asked to question the tramps.

"Did they give you any trouble, Sheriff?"

"No, not at all. They claim they haven't done

anything but were glad to be out of the cold. Your wire didn't say why you're looking for them. What is it they're suspected of?"

Hodgins sat in the chair in front of the Sheriff's desk, dropping his bag at his feet.

"There was a murder the other day and they were seen in the vicinity. I'm not saying they did it, but they may have seen something. They left town right after, which would normally be suspicious, but they're tramps so it's not unusual for them to be travelling."

"Rather odd to see a white man travelling with a coloured one, so I knew who you were looking for right off. They've been through here before and no one ever had any complaints about them. They're both skilled carpenters. Could make a good living if they chose to stay in one place."

A gust of cold wind burst through the room when the front door opened. A scrawny woman Hodgins guessed to be in her forties came in and sat a basket on the desk.

"Breakfast for your guests as ordered. Little late, but I've been busy." She drew back the cloth covering the contents, revealing two thick slices of bread and a couple of pieces of ham. Steam rose from the freshly baked bread, filling the air with a mouth-watering aroma.

"Thank you, Daisy. Don't suppose you could spare a

few more slices for two famished lawmen?"

Daisy put her hands where her hips would be if she had any substance to her. "Why the devil didn't ya ask for more in the first place? Person could catch their death going in and out of the cold." She wrapped her shawl around her head and continued to grumble as she stomped out the door, slamming it behind her.

"Woman's never happier than when she's got something to complain about." Sheriff Davidson picked up the basket and headed to the back. "Help yourself to the coffee. It's not the best tasting, but it's nice and hot."

Hodgins found a reasonably clean cup and filled it with the dark liquid. It was stronger than he was used to, but it warmed his insides. The fire was low, so he took it upon himself to add another log. It crackled and popped as it provided much needed warmth. Davidson returned, retrieved the empty cup that sat on his desk and joined Hodgins.

"I've not had occasion to come out this way before. Based on the name, I'm guessing there are a lot of German's in the area."

They moved over to the Sheriff's desk before continuing their conversation. Davidson leaned back, his bulk causing the chair to groan as he put his boots up on the desk. "The area was first settled by Mennonites. Didn't get the Germans until after the Napoleonic wars. We've quite the assortment of skilled tradesmen here. Food's not bad either. Still prefer my wife's steak, eggs, and bread through." He glanced down at Hodgins' carryall. "Planning on staying awhile?"

"Not sure. Feels like there's a storm brewing so I thought I'd come prepared."

"There's a clean boarding house down the street, run by our charming Miss Daisy."

Another rush of cold air brought a second basket from Daisy, still grumbling. They ate in silence, Hodgins hungrier then he'd realized, the food in his bag long forgotten. Once the ham and bread were consumed, Hodgins stood.

"Guess I'd better speak to the two men now."

Davidson showed Hodgins to the back where the tramps were, retrieved the now empty basket, then went back to his desk.

When Hodgins saw the two tramps, their appearance surprised him. Instead of a pair of weather old men as he'd expected, they were relatively young. The negro wore a straw hat, dirty brown pants and was probably about thirty-five, while the other was maybe still in his twenties. Both stood and politely greeted the detective. Hodgins noticed the negro was bow-legged and stood several inches shorter than his own six-foot two frame. If not for the bowed legs, Hodgins guessed he'd be his height. He tried not to laugh as he wondered if the negro's weight made his legs bow so much. The white tramp, however, towered over him. He had hair as red as Doctor McKenzie's and spoke with a thick Scottish accent.

"People call me Scotty. My friend here goes by Curly." Both tramps laughed at the joke as the negro didn't have a hair on his head. Hodgins thought it peculiar that the men would be so jovial after being arrested. Maybe they weren't guilty of anything and it was just a coincidence they'd been seen in the area Friday evening. He took an instant liking to them.

Curly spoke first. "Not that I'm complaining to have a roof over my head and a hot meal in my belly, but what's we locked up for?"

"I need to know where you were last Friday evening."

Scotty and Curley looked at each other, shoulders raised, heads shaking.

"We dinnae have much occasion to take notice of the day or time," Scotty answered.

"No, I don't suppose you do. Maybe it would help if I told you that you both were seen in Toronto and caught trying to hop a train."

"Toronto? Yes, we visited your fair city recently,"

Curly said.

"If you don't mind me saying, you both sound fairly well spoken for a pair of tramps."

"Ah, yes." Curly spoke up first. "I spent my younger days in the employ of a fine gentleman in the south. He insisted I had some learning and conduct myself appropriately. When I left after the old gent passed away, I found it to my advantage to continue so. Folks are less leery when you sound educated, especially when you don't look like them."

Hodgins turned to the young Scotsman. "And you?"

"Spent a few years at the University in Glasgow before I plucked up the courage to leave. Was nae interested in following in me father's footsteps. No interest in business, but I enjoy working with my hands." He nodded towards Curly. "We met by chance on a train from New York City a few years ago and have travelled together since."

Both men seemed to Hodgins to be quite content with their chosen path. He couldn't image either harming anyone. "Do you recall what you did while in Toronto? Anything at all?"

The stocky negro sat back on the cot and leaned against the wall. "Let me think. Spent some time on a farm. Helped build a lean-to on the back of the house.

Babe on the way and they needed more room. Scotty fixed the cradle the man tried to build." He slapped his knee and barked out a laugh. "Sorriest cradle I ever did see."

"Aye. I would nae put a dead dog in something so wobbly. The misses was so pleased she packed enough food for a couple of days when we left. We went through the city on the way to the station. If you say that was Friday, then I will nae disagree."

Hodgins made notes in his little book. "Don't suppose you know the name of the farmer?"

"Don't have much need for names," Curly replied.

"Suppose you also don't have much need to recall where they lived either?"

Both shook their heads. "North of the city is all I can tell you," Scotty said. "Took the better part of a day to reach the train."

"North, right." Hodgins wrote that down and wondered how long it would take to find the right farm.

The land north of the city was sparsely settled, small settlements dotted along the more highly travelled carriageways, numerous farms on the outskirts of each town. Maybe someone would know a family about to have a baby. Hodgins flipped through his notes. "Some people saw you near Ketchum School. What were you doing there? Said you were arguing."

The two tramps looked at each other and shrugged. "Don't know nothin' 'bout a school, but we did have a lively conversation or two," Curley said.

"Large brick building near the north end of Toronto, park and woods beside it," Hodgins prompted.

"Aye, I believe I know where you mean," Scotty said. He turned to Curly. "That'd be where we *discussed* which direction to go next."

"That's right. I remember now. Is that why we're locked up? Is it a crime to argue with a friend?"

"No," Hodgins said. "Man was found murdered on the school grounds."

Neither man seemed surprised. "We saw no one, Detective. The streets were empty when we went by," Curly said.

"And we killed no one," Scotty added. He held up his calloused hands "These hands bring wood to life, not take life from the living."

Hodgins had no reason to either believe or disbelieve the tramps, but his instinct said to believe them. He had no witnesses to the crime and no evidence pointing to anyone, except his brother.

He sighed and left the back room, not bothering to close the cell door.

"May as well release them, Sheriff. But ask them to

stay in town."

"You don't think they're responsible then? Good. I could use their carpentry skills myself. Wife's been at me to fix some things, and the weather does feel like it's going to take a bad turn. I can probably keep them busy for a few weeks. Meals and lodgings in exchange for work."

As Hodgins was reasonably satisfied the tramps weren't responsible, and the sheriff would be keeping an eye on them, he decided not to stay over in Berlin. The next train back was at 3:37. He checked his pocket watch. Plenty of time before it pulled out, so he stayed and chatted with Davidson, even treated him to a meal.

When they left the restaurant, the air was noticeably colder. He bade the Sheriff farewell and rushed to the train station, the German food not quite settled in his stomach. He was glad he didn't have to stay over, and would be back home in time to enjoy his wife's Irish cooking. Once he was settled on the train, he pulled out his little notebook and reviewed the few bits of information he had.

Brown died Friday early evening according to McKenzie, but his body wasn't found until mid-morning Saturday. He'd been left out in the open, so why wasn't he discovered earlier? Maybe the cold weather had led the coroner to be mistaken about the time of death. The only possible suspects were the tramps and his own brother. He believed the story the tramps relayed, and Jonathan hadn't even arrived in Toronto when Brown had been killed.

The amount of blood around the body left no doubt in Hodgins' mind that Brown died at the school. Someone must have heard the shot. The area around Ketchum School was quiet and the sound of a guns firing would have carried. Either he'd missed speaking with one of the neighbours or somebody lied. Reading back over the interviews with the people around the school, Hodgins realized one of the houses on Bishop Street had been empty the first time they checked with the neighbours around the school, and he hadn't gone back. He made a note to try the house again and to check with Barnes to see if any of the homes he visited also had no answer. Hodgins closed his notebook, then dug out the lunch Cordelia packed, hoping the biscuits would help settle his stomach.

CHAPTER TEN

When Hodgins arrived back at Station House Number Four, Barnes practically knocked him over in his rush to speak with the detective.

"Slow down, lad. Let me get my overcoat off and a cup of hot tea. Whatever it is can wait another few minutes."

Hodgins stood in front of the wood stove briefly, enjoying the heat emanating through the vents. After hanging his overcoat on a nearby peg, he went into the back and fixed a cup of tea. He noticed Barnes pacing in front of his office when he came back out front.

"All right. You look like you're about ready to burst. What is it?"

Barnes followed Hodgins into his office. "While you were away, a wire came in from Montréal. Apparently, a man walked into one of their police stations and confessed to killing Brown. They're already on the way here with him. Should arrive around 11:30 tonight."

"Well, that saves us a lot of bother. We can

concentrate on something else if we've got the killer. Jonathan will be happy to hear that bit of news, too. Strange how that man just up and confessed. Why flee to another province, someplace we're not even looking, and go to the police? He's not someone we've been searching for, whoever he is. Probably would've gotten away with it if he'd kept his gob shut."

"It is puzzling, sir." Barnes sat opposite the detective and laid a paper on the desk. "Here's the wire. Guess you made the trip to Berlin for naught."

Hodgins finished his tea and leaned back. "Suppose. I wasn't totally convinced those two were guilty anyway. They could've travelled a lot farther if they wanted to escape getting caught. Pleasant enough chaps, and Sheriff Davidson said they'd been there before and had no trouble with them. Need to confirm their whereabouts, just in case. Brown wasn't overly large, but he was strong. Not convinced one man could subdue him, and it could just as easily been three men arguing, not two. The argument may not even be relevant."

Hodgins asked Barnes to fetch a few of the other constables before they left. Barnes corralled four of them before they had a chance to leave. They all crowded into Hodgins' office.

"I know the weather's getting bad, but I need you to

visit the farms north of the city first thing tomorrow. Get yourselves horses from the livery and bundle up. I need you to find the farm where two tramps did some work last week. Young couple, wife's with child. About a days walk from the city. Might be a bit further. Don't go too far out, and for God's sake, if the weather gets worse, turn back."

Hodgins gave them a description of the tramps and sent them home. He retrieved the wire from Boston to re-read the incident between Jonathan and Janel Brown. Not a lot of detail had been provided. The end of the wire said details would be sent by post. Hodgins wasn't certain he wanted to read it when it arrived.

"Barnes, I believe I'll go see what my beautiful wife is fixing for supper. It's past your time as well. I'll meet the train tonight, personally."

* * *

After supper, Sara played in the sitting room, so Hodgins didn't get the opportunity to speak with Jonathan about the wire, but did mention the prisoner coming in on the train.

"Looks like you've been given an early Christmas present," Hodgins said. "We'll know more after I interview him. I'll get him settled into a nice cold cell tonight, then interrogate him first thing."

The evening dragged on, but the time finally came to

meet the late train. Hodgins was surprised when he opened his front door and encountered a foot or more of snow.

"Blast." He turned up the collar on his overcoat and ran up the street to where a carriage stood. He slipped a few times but managed to stay on his feet. The driver was brushing snow off one of the black horses. Hodgins ran his hand over the other horse to clear the snow from it's back and to hurry the driver along.

"Done for the night, sir. Have to find another."

Hodgins showed his badge. "One more trip. Need to get to Union Station. Wait for me. I'll be coming back with two more passengers after the train arrives."

The train was a half-hour late. The horses stomped their large feet and snorted, anxious to get moving. As the train pulled out, Hodgins led the Montréal policeman and his prisoner to the waiting carriage. The two men were groggy, barely able to stay awake. The officer said little, speaking in broken English. "The train, how you say? Wobbly?"

Hodgins smiled. "I believe you mean rickety." He wiggled his hand up and down. The officer nodded.

"Oui, rickety."

"I'm afraid the cab ride won't be much smoother, but at least it's quiet."

The officer got in first. Hodgins helped the

handcuffed prisoner up, seating him beside the Montréal policeman before settling on the seat opposite. Both the prisoner and accompanying officer were half asleep and dozed off in the carriage, despite the bumps and cold.

Hodgins studied the prisoner while he slept: a toad of a man with a receding hairline and bulging eyes. Hodgins wondered how he could have over-powered Brown. When they arrived back at Station Four, he once again asked the driver to wait, offering him the comfort of the police livery. The officer from Montréal asked if he could spend the night in one of the empty cells as he was leaving on the first train out and didn't want to go back out in the cold to find a room.

"No need to sleep in a cold cell. We have a small cot in the back, near the pot belly stove. Nice and warm. You can help yourself to tea, and you'll find some biscuits in a tin."

Once the prisoner was locked up, Hodgins showed the officer where he could sleep.

I didn't get your name," Hodgins said.

"Jean Beaudoin, Sargent De Police." He extended a hand as he yawned.

"Albert Hodgins. Thank you for coming so quickly."

"Ah, my son, he is Albert." He yawned again.

"I'm keeping you up. Make yourself comfortable."

Hodgins pointed to a shelf over a small sink. "Tea and biscuits are up there. Good night."

Hodgins hurried to the livery, anxious to climb into his own bed. He couldn't stop thinking about the prisoner. There was no way he could've dragged a dead body alone, especially so far, and in the snow. The area where the bloodied branch was found had to be at least three hundred feet from the school. He must have had help. Could he be wrong thinking the tramps were not involved?

As the streets were deserted at such a late hour, Hodgins arrived home in no time. The driver spoke sharply when he halted the horses.

"Yer home, sir. And that's where I'm headed myself."

Feeling guilty for detaining the driver more than two hours, Hodgins gave him a generous tip, earning him a nod and smile.

CHAPTER ELEVEN

Once again Hodgins woke to find himself behind his time. It was almost nine when he hurried into the kitchen. Jonathan sat enjoying a cup of tea with a constable, but not Barnes. That new constable again, Harry? No, Perry. Hodgins raised an eyebrow when he recognized the lad.

"I hope you're not here to tell me there's another body at the school."

"No, sir. Not that I know of. Inspector sent me in to find you. Wants you at the station right away."

"Tell him I'll see him when I can. I have a prisoner to interrogate. Tell him we may have caught the killer."

"Yes, sir." The constable rose to leave.

"Finish your tea. It's cold outside."

The constable remained standing and gulped down the contents of his cup, then scurried out the door after thanking Cordelia.

"That should keep the Inspector satisfied for a little while. I suspect he wants an update for the Chief Inspector and Gruger. I've been putting it off for too long. Hopefully, after interrogating the man brought in last night I'll be able to tell him we have the culprit." He turned to his wife. "Delia, I'm famished. Fix me up a large helping of eggs and sausages if you don't mind. Meanwhile, I'll just start with some of these." Hodgins uncovered the basket that sat on the table and took out two of the steaming hot biscuits, then, as usual, slathered them with her homemade apply jelly.

"Shouldn't you be hurrying along?" Cordelia remarked.

Hodgins took a large bite of his biscuit before answering. "Mouth watering, my dear." He took another bite. "I have a prisoner that needs questioning. Can't do that properly on an empty stomach now, can I? As long as the constable tells the Inspector that we may have the killer, he'll be content enough to wait."

Jonathan and Cordelia exchanged puzzled looks. It wasn't like Hodgins to be so unconcerned.

"Hurry along Delia. I'd like to have my breakfast before lunch time." He winked and shoved the rest of the biscuit in his mouth.

Delia smiled and went over to the cold box for three eggs and some sausages. Jonathan made himself another cup of tea. "This chap, he went all the way to Montréal before confessing?"

"Yes. Strange that, don't you agree? Why travel all the way to Montréal? Why the devil didn't he come to one of the stations here in Toronto?"

"Who knows how someone's mind works? Maybe sitting on the train, his conscience got the better of him. Maybe he's a simpleton. I'm certain you'll beat it out of him."

Hodgins glared at his brother. "I do *not* beat my prisoners. I realize that's a common practice, but in my experience, all it does is make an innocent man confess just to make it stop. Then the real culprit gets away. I strongly urge all my men not to resort to extreme force. Unfortunately, I can't stop them unless I'm in the room with them. I'll admit I've hit a few myself, but I've never beaten anyone."

The conversation stopped when Cordelia sat a plate loaded with scrambled eggs and sausages in front of her husband. She cleared the dirty tea cups off the table, washed and put them away while he ate in silence. The scent of the sausages didn't even rouse the sleeping dog. When Hodgins finished, he took his plate to the sink, kissed Delia on the cheek, then turned to Jonathan.

"Once your family is settled in after the long train ride, what's say we go out and cut down a tree? This will be our first Christmas in our new house and we must have the biggest and best tree we can find. I have Sunday off. I'll hire a cutter sleigh and we'll head out to the country after church. Stop somewhere for a bite to eat. Make a day of it. Did you have a chance to look at that bit I tore from the paper about Rip van Winkle at the Opera House?"

"I'm certain the children would enjoy both that and cutting a tree," Jonathan said.

"Yes, that sounds lovely, dear," Cordelia added.

"Speaking of children, where's Sara?" Hodgins asked.

"She's gone skating with her friend Lucy. She was ever so excited about cutting down a tree and wanted to make certain her friend knows all about it."

"Do you have anywhere in mind to find a nice tree?" Jonathan asked.

Hodgins tapped the side of his nose and smiled. "Can't give away any secrets. I'll try not to be late," he said, heading for the front door.

* * *

Hodgins stood outside the interrogation room, watching the suspect through a rip in the curtains. The fabric wasn't thick, but it allowed privacy when someone felt it necessary to get rough or to hide the identity of a witness. The man sat hunched over the table, sweat beading on his brow despite the chilly weather. Somehow, he seemed even smaller than the night before.

"How the hell did a man of such a small stature overpower a street-wise and strong man like Brown?"

The constable standing beside him shrugged in reply. Hodgins had been thinking about that all the way to the station. He watched the man fidget in the chair. Nervous sort of chap. How could he pluck up the courage to murder anyone? He opened the door and went in, taking a seat on the opposite side of the table.

"Mr. Towers, I understand you've confessed to killing someone in Toronto. Is that correct?"

Towers drummed the edge of the table with his fingers, staring at a scar on the tabletop. "Yes," he whispered.

"Tell me what happened. Why did you kill him? Start from the beginning."

"Made me angry, so I shot him." He stopped after just one sentence.

"And" Hodgins prompted. "Made you mad how?"

"Um, owed me money. Said he didn't have it so I shot him."

"I see. And after you shot him, did you check to see if he had your money on him?"

Towers nodded. "Checked his pockets. Empty."

First lie.

"Where did you shoot him?"

"In the school yard."

"No, I mean where on his person."

Towers scrunched his face as though trying to retrieve a memory. "Head, shot him in the head."

"Funny that," Hodgins said. "His bowler never even fell off."

"Put it back on him."

Second lie.

The questioning continued for over thirty minutes. Hodgins would ask a question and receive little more than a one-sentence answer. His frustration grew along with the serious doubts as to Towers' guilt.

"Tell me again, where in the head did you shoot him?"

"Left side, like the paper said."

Hodgins slammed his palms on the table and stood, his chair scrapping the wooden floor. "I knew it." Towers had not told him anything that hadn't already been in the newspapers. "You odious little toad. You're not guilty of anything except wasting everyone's time. I ought to lock you up for interfering in our investigation."

Towers slunk down in the chair and almost slid under the table.

"Constable," Hodgins yelled. "Get this worthless

piece of shite out of my sight." Hodgins stepped back, sending his chair toppling over.

The door opened and the constable who brought Towers up from the cells entered. "Want me ta lock him back up?"

"No. Throw him out. He's no more guilty that I am. What a waste of time. I'm sure the police in Montréal won't be pleased to know one of their own wasted two days for nothing. Is Sergeant Beaudoin still here?"

"Left about an hour ago."

Hodgins slapped his hands on the table again, leaning towards Towers. "I don't want to see you in my police station ever again. Do you understand?"

Towers nodded and without waiting for the constable to escort him, bolted out the door and through the station house. Barnes grabbed him when Towers rushed past.

"Let him go," Hodgins said. "Nothing more than an attention seeker."

Barnes released him and the man hurried out into the cold. Hodgins slammed the door to his office and kicked his chair before sitting. Barnes lightly tapped on the glass and waited. Hodgins hesitated before waving him in.

"Why did you let him go, sir?"

"That little toad just wanted some attention. Suppose it made him feel important. Read about it in the paper and decided to confess. God only knows why. Now we're back where we started. The only suspects are those two tramps and my brother, and I don't believe any of them are guilty. We've hit one dead end after another. Someone has to be lying and I don't want to believe it's my brother. Maybe I was wrong to dismiss the tramps so soon. Just because they were pleasant doesn't mean they didn't do it. What about the search for the farm couple. Any luck?"

"Four constables went out first thing. Two have already returned. Schancy came across a doctor who thinks he knows the couple. He's going back out with a fresh horse to find the farm. Should know soon if it's the right one."

"Hope it doesn't take long. The wind and snow started again a little while ago. Don't want to have to send out a search party for my men. Feels like it's going to be bad when it hits. With any luck it'll wait until after my sister-in-law arrives." He checked the time. "I best be going home. Entire family's going to meet the train. Imagine, four adults, three children, armfuls of gifts, and one very large dog, all under one roof. May have to evict a few mice to make more room."

"I envy you, sir. This will be the first Christmas without my pa. We've been invited to the Halloway's for Christmas dinner, but I dare say it won't be as lively as your home is bound to be."

"Why don't you and your family drop by, if you've no other plans? Christmas Eve maybe, or Boxing Day?

Barnes' solemn face lit up. "Why that's right nice of you, sir. I know Ma isn't planning anything, but I don't know about Violet. She may have plans that she hasn't told me about yet."

"By all means, bring your fiancée and her parents."

Barnes blushed, but smiled. "Haven't asked her yet."

Hodgins waved a hand dismissively. "She'll say yes, don't you worry about that."

"Are you certain Mrs. Hodgins won't mind? No offence, but your home isn't terribly large."

Hodgins laughed. "We'll fit everyone in somehow. Delia won't mind. She loves a party. I'll mention it today. Besides, she'll have Jonathan's wife, Elizabeth, to help." He rose from his chair and walked to the office door. "Let me know when Schancy has news. I'll go upstairs and give the Inspector the bad news about Towers before leaving to pick up Jonathan's family. Train's due at two. If anything new turns up, I'll either be at Union Station or at home."

Hodgins stopped at Grand's livery on Bay Street before going home to reserve two of their best carriages. The two-seat cabriolets just wouldn't be near large enough for everyone and their baggage.

CHAPTER TWELVE

"Six more people?" Delia faced Hodgins, hands on her hips. "How am I supposed to fit all those people around our table?"

"Doesn't have to be a sit-down dinner party. Just friends and family enjoying some time together. I didn't think you'd mind. Are you terribly angry? Nothing's set. I can always un-invite them."

Delia's mouth opened in horror. "Albert Hodgins, don't you dare un-invite them. And no, I'm not angry. You just caught me by surprise. Now that I think about it, it would be nice. Let me mull it over." She looked at the tall clock in the hallway. "Is that the time? Gracious, we'll be late meeting the train." Delia rushed upstairs to make sure Sara was getting ready.

"You're a lucky man," Jonathan said. "My Elizabeth would have had fits if I sprang something like that on her."

"If they were coming tonight I'd get a right earful for certain. At least there's no date set so she has almost two weeks to plan and shop. She actually enjoys all the fuss and bother. If there was a possibility she could plan parties for a living, I'm positive she'd do just that."

The brothers moved into the sitting room to wait for the carriages to arrive. Scraps padded along and flopped in front of the fire, all four legs sticking out. Jonathan reached down and scratched top of Scraps' head.

"Must be exhausting laying around the house all day. I'd have taken him for a walk earlier but the weather was too nasty."

Hodgins poured them both a whisky and they sat in the chairs by the fire. Jonathan leaned back and stretched out his legs.

"I suppose you've got this murder all wrapped up, what with that chap confessing."

Hodgins threw back his head, downing the whisky. "No, afraid not. Turns out he just read about it. Don't understand why some folk feel the need to confess to a crime they didn't commit. Especially when it results in a dance at the end of a rope."

Jonathan stared at his whisky, fingers silently tapping the glass. "Does that move me back to the top of the suspect list?" He looked up at his brother without raising his head.

"No." The word came out slow, as though he still gave it thought. "I'm at a loss. The two tramps seem to have a witness for their whereabouts. Just waiting for confirmation. Looks like I'll have to head back to Aurora, once the weather clears."

Delia and Sara were half-way down the stairs when someone knocked on the door. Sara ran to open it before anyone else. Two carriages sat in front of the house; one led by a pair of chestnut horses, the other by a pair of greys.

"Hurry, Daddy, Uncle Jon. Get your coats. We'll be late."

"We've plenty of time, Sara." Hodgins pinched her nose. "Get your coat and hat on. Bundle up. It's going to be a cold ride."

Sara grabbed Jonathan's hand and dragged him out the door before he had time to button his coat. "I'll ride with you, Uncle Jon. Keep you from being lonely." She raced out to the street and the driver of the greys helped her up.

"There you go miss. Here's a warm wool blanket for your legs."

Cordelia and Hodgins got in the other carriage and the horses made their way down Avenue Road, across Bloor to Yonge, then down to Union Station. The train was just pulling in when they arrived. Jonathan looked up and down the platform, searching for his family.

"There they are." He pointed down the platform and waved. "Elizabeth!" He stopped a porter and helped him load a cart with their trunks and boxes.

"Is this all?" he joked. The baggage cart was so full the porter had to give it an extra shove to get it going. The cart slide sideways on the freshly fallen snow that begun just before the train pulled in. Another porter rushed to sweep off the platform while Hodgins reached out, preventing the cart from hitting Cordelia.

"I thought I'd finish the Christmas shopping here."

Hodgins noticed his brothers' sarcasm was lost on Elizabeth.

"Children, I want you to meet your Aunt Cordelia and Uncle Albert. And this lovely girl must be Sara." She gave her children a gentle push. "Cora, Freddie, this is your cousin Sara."

"I've so many things planned for us to do," Sara said. "We'll have so much fun."

"Don't you have any other children?" Freddie asked. "Just a girl?"

Hodgins laughed. "Sorry, but you'll have to make do. We men are rather out numbered. At least Scraps is a boy."

"Who's Scraps?" Freddie asked.

"We have a dog and he's ever so large," Sara

answered. "He a very clever dog. Saved Daddy's life."

Freddie's eyes widened "Gosh, no fooling?"

"No fooling," Hodgins said.

As they followed the porter out to their carriages, a burst of steam shot out from the train, causing Elizabeth's skirt to wrap around her legs. "Can we please get away from this disgustingly dirty train?"

Hodgins heard a tiny giggle escape from Cordelia. He'd forgotten how prissy Elizabeth could be. It seemed she'd gotten worse. No wonder she and Jonathan separated briefly.

"Why don't we get everything in the carriages and I'll tell you all about our hairy hero after we get home," Hodgins said.

CHAPTER THIRTEEN

When they arrived home, Hodgins and Jonathan helped the drivers unload the baggage and parcels that filled both carriages. Cordelia showed Elizabeth and the children their rooms, leaving them to unpack and settle in, then headed to the kitchen. She had planned an elaborate meal to welcome her in-laws and wanted to get it started.

Earlier in the day, she'd purchased a large roast, big enough to last for several meals. There were still a few carrots, beets, and potatoes left from her modest harvest a few months earlier. Even though her husband had dug out a patch in the back, it wasn't nearly large enough to grow sufficient quantities to see them through the winter. At least she'd been able to save some of the household money to put towards a few Christmas treats.

The men stayed out of the everyone's way and resumed their conversation in the sitting room.

"Do you think you'll find anything useful up in Aurora? You mentioned that ropemaker. Could someone from there be responsible?"

Hodgins refilled his glass with whisky before sitting down.

"I honestly don't know. I had hoped to get back up there today to talk to more people. My list of suspects is rather short."

"Don't remind me." Jonathan laughed nervously.

"It's not funny, brother. How am I to remain impartial? I can't step aside. I've been directed to handle this personally. I don't want my older brother to be guilty, and the thought of someone randomly killing people around the city is terrifying."

"Just be thankful it's only one person and not a string of them. I give you my word, I did *not* kill Brown, but I'd like to shake the hand of the man who did."

"From what I've read in the report the Boston police sent, I imagine quite a number of people would join you in a que for that. Feel sorry for his wife. She'll have her hands full with three little ones."

Jonathan choked on his whisky at the mention of Janel Brown. "You've met her?"

"Yes, when I went up to Aurora, Tuesday."

"You have to admit she's a beautiful woman. Won't be unwed long, I'm sure."

"Not many men are willing to take on a widow with

children, especially young babies. But yes, I agree, she's a looker. Even disheveled and tired as she was, her beauty was evident." Hodgins reached over the arm of his chair and sat his empty glass on the floor. "She's got freckles across her nose, much like my Delia, and she's the most intriguing shade of green eyes. Yes, I'm sure she'll be wed again. Hopefully she makes a better selection next time."

Freddie charged into the room and dropped to his knees beside the resting dog. Scraps' tail thumped against the rug and he rolled over on his back.

"May I pat him, Daddy?" he pleaded.

"You'll have to ask your uncle. It is his dog after all."

Freddie turned to Hodgins, hand hovering over Scraps' belly.

"Go ahead. When the girls come down, why don't you all go into the yard and play with him?"

"Oh, that would be splendid fun." He giggled as Scraps licked his hand, then laid beside the dog and stroked Scraps' belly while waiting for Cora to finished unpacking. It wasn't long before the girls came down. The children put on their coats and boots and ran out the back door with Scraps leading the way into the yard.

Jonathan retrieved the newspaper from the mantle and gave part of it to his brother. "No more talk of murder, at least not today."

"Agreed." Hodgins took the pages and settled back in his chair.

* * *

Hodgins watched as Cordelia sat in front of her mirrored dressing table, removing the pins from her hair, placing them in a small porcelain dish.

"It's been a most tiring day, Bertie. I'm certain to fall asleep as soon as my head touches the pillow, if not sooner." She picked up her silver-handled brush and began the nightly ritual. Fifty strokes down the left side of her waist-long red hair, and fifty down the right, followed by a single loose braid, tied with a ribbon.

Hodgins hung his jacket in the armoire, then unbuttoned his shirt. Cordelia watched his reflection in the mirror of her dressing table.

"You've seemed troubled all evening, Bertie. Is it the man found at Sara's school? You haven't spoken much of it."

Hodgins sighed and sat on the edge of the bed. "I don't know what to do. Jonathan is at the top of my suspect list, such as it is. If he was anyone else, I'd have him in my jail."

Delia stopped braiding and turned to face him. "Jonathan? How can you possibly think he's responsible? What haven't you told me?"

"It's been difficult to speak about it with him in the house. Where do I start?"

"At the beginning, naturally." Delia finished braiding her hair and joined him on the edge of the bed. "Why do you think Jonathan is responsible? Surely not because he had a dalliance with the man's wife?"

"He didn't have a dalliance, at least he said it went no further than a few comments. It's everything. He knew Brown before, fired him for theft, tried to get familiar with his wife, was beaten up by Brown and his associates, and Jonathan's business card was found on the body. Is it a coincidence Brown was murdered just when Jonathan came to town?"

Delia thought for a moment, silently ticking off items on her fingers. "Didn't you say this Brown fellow was murdered early Friday evening?"

Hodgins nodded.

"But Jonathan arrived just before midnight on Friday."

"That's the only reason he hasn't been arrested. But I've been thinking about that. I didn't actually see him get off the train. I've been putting off confirming it. If it were anyone else, I'd have asked to see his ticket and checked with rail employees."

"Didn't you tell me earlier there was an envelope of

money in Brown's pocket? Could an associate have done it and been scared off before he had time to search his pockets?"

"The thought crossed my mind. Brown had quite the collection of dubious associates. I need to make more inquires. If the weather clears by Monday, I'll be taking the train back to Aurora to ask around."

But if Brown is from Boston and only recently moved up here, who would he know well enough to want him dead?"

Hodgins thought a moment. "Good point, Delia. It generally takes a lengthy hate to want to kill someone."

"Could it simply be mistaken identity?"

"Why, I hadn't even considered that. It was dark, difficult to make out features. I suppose he could have been clubbed from behind, then shot. But why not leave him in the trees? Why go to the bother of dragging him over to the school? It's as though he was placed there for a reason. Trouble is, I can't for the life of me figure out what that reason is." He sighed. "More questions than answers I'm afraid."

He kissed her cheek. "I think it's time you retired for the night. You look like you're ready to drop. With three children in the house, you'll need all the rest you can get."

As Delia crawled under the flannel blankets she

muttered, "Don't forget about the dog. He'll be extra rambunctious," the final word slipped out, barely more than a whisper.

CHAPTER FOURTEEN

The storm hit its peak overnight and continued all through Saturday before going on its way, leaving everything covered in clean, white fluff. When Hodgins looked out Sunday morning, at least three inches of snow clung to the bare branches of the maples and oaks, and the evergreen branches drooped under the extra weight. He heard Delia fussing in the kitchen and turned away from the upstairs window. He dressed quickly and went down to light the fire in the sitting room. The back door latch clicked, followed shortly by a not-too-gentle slam. Curious, he went into the kitchen and found Delia staring out the window. Peering over the top of her head, he could see Scraps running around the snow-family the children built the previous evening. They were buried up to what would be their knees, if they had any. Scraps ran circles around them, then rolled in the snow, knocking one of the smaller snow people over. The head landed on the dog, sending him in more circles.

"I'd better get him in before he's completely covered.

That shaggy coat will take forever to dry." Hodgins went into the small enclosed back porch and called the dog. The breeze that came in didn't have the same bite to it as the last several days. When Scraps spotted his favourite human he raced to the door. Hodgins had an old blanket ready and managed to wrap the dog before the beast's hairy paws soaked his suit jacket and vest. After rubbing the dog down as best he could, they both went inside. Scraps went straight to his blanket by the wood stove.

"Look at all those tiny balls of snow on his undercoat. That blanket will be soaked once they melt," Delia remarked.

"Packing snow. I'd better get a start cleaning the front walk. It's going to be the devil to move. With all this snow, the buggies and carriages will have trouble moving. It feels quite mild, though, so what say we walk to church? It's not that far and will probably be quicker."

* * *

After church, the children rushed to change out of their Sunday clothing, anxious to go looking for a tree. Hodgins broke the news when they came back downstairs, "I'm sorry Sara, but it will have to wait for another day. There's just too much snow. Plenty of time yet."

Sara pouted. "But you promised we'd get the tree today."

"Sara," Delia scolded. "Don't speak to your father like that. He can't control the weather. When the roads clear, we'll go and cut a tree. Now, why don't you and your cousins make some decorations?"

"Can we string popcorn?" Freddie asked. "I helped Mama last Christmas."

"I'm afraid we don't have any corn for popping just yet, but we've lots of coloured paper and glue. Why not make some chains after lunch?"

Once everyone was fed and the dishes put away, Albert and Jonathan retired to the sitting room to read and stay out of the way. The children busied themselves cutting strips of paper and gluing together chains, tree forgotten. Delia took Elizabeth into the sewing room to show her the dresses she was making for Sara. Scraps' head rose and he suddenly bolted off his blanket and raced down the hall, wagging his tail and barking. Someone knocked on the front door.

Hodgins rose to see who it was while Jonathan went to the bay window. "Looks like you're going to work."

Hodgins opened the front door to let the constable in.

"Sorry to disturb you, but there's been another murder." Barnes gulped several times, trying to catch his breath.

"Not at the school again, I hope?"

"No. This one was left in the laneway right behind the station house, sitting up and blindfolded, just like Brown."

"I can tell by the look on your face there's more to it."

Barnes reached into his pocket and pulled out a card. He hesitated before handing it over.

"Damnation!"

"Problem brother?" Jonathan stood behind Hodgins. "Afternoon Constable."

"Someone's left a body near my station house." He held the card up so Jonathan could read it. "This is your new business address, is it not?"

* * *

The detective and his brother once again stood beside a metal table in the coroner's office. Hodgins placed a hand on Jonathan's shoulder and faced Dr. McKenzie. "Sorry to disturb you on a Sunday."

McKenzie waved his hand, dismissing the comment. "Just like last time. He'll look like he's asleep. Except for a small hole over the left eye."

Jonathan swayed and his brother supported him.

"Steady on. Ready?"

Jonathan took a deep breath and closed his eyes.

"Ready as I'll ever be."

McKenzie lowered the sheet to expose the man's head. "Recognize him?"

Jonathan opened one eye and glanced down. "Yes. It's George Roberts. Associate of Brown." He turned away. "He's one of the men I fired for theft."

"That was before you moved. Why would he have your new card?" Hodgins asked.

"They were printed in advance. He could have taken one before I had the books checked."

The detective turned to the coroner. "Doctor, do you know when this Roberts fellow died?"

"Can't pinpoint exact time because of the cold, but he couldn't have been there long, else someone would have found him sooner."

"True. It's a popular shortcut, especially for some of my lads. One of them would have seen a body on their way in or out if he'd been left last night. Let me know when you've finished your examination. It can wait until tomorrow."

Hodgins turned back to his brother. "I need to speak with the person who found him. Are you well enough to make it home?"

"I'm not a baby, Albert. I'm perfectly capable of making my way back to your house."

He took a step towards the door and swayed again, reaching for the doctor's desk for support. "Think I'll hail a hansom."

Hodgins stood with his brother until an empty cab came. He recognized the driver. "Take my brother to my home, will you Peter? He's not feeling well." Hodgins chuckled as he walked to the station.

* * *

The station house was almost empty when Hodgins arrived. Most of the officers were out on their beats, except Barnes, who looked up when the front door opened, and one of the new recruits. A young couple in their early twenties sat at the constable's desk. Both looked to be in shock, the young woman sobbing.

"That the couple who found him?" Hodgins asked Barnes.

"Yes, they were out for a stroll after church. Decided to take a shortcut down the lane and found him. They've made a statement, and I've sent someone to fetch their parents."

"Fine. Bring me their statements." He went into his office and removed his overcoat. Barnes rushed in as Hodgins pulled the chair away from his desk.

"It's rather short." Barnes handed the sheets to Hodgins.

"Understandable." He sat down and indicated for Barnes to sit as well. "Give it a day or so and talk to the young man again. See if he remembers anything new." He read through the statements. "How much snow was on the body? It doesn't say."

"Snow? Didn't notice any. Is that important?"

"Is it important? Of course it is. Dr. McKenzie can't give us a very accurate time of death because of the cold weather. When did it stop snowing?"

"Sometime early this morning I believe." Barnes snapped his fingers. "Of course. If the body had been left during the night it would have been completely covered."

"Good man. Knew you'd figure it out."

"Wish I was as quick as you, sir. Just not smart enough I suppose."

"Balderdash. You're more than smart enough. Leaps and bounds over most of the constables here. Sergeant, too, but I won't admit to ever saying that."

Barnes seemed flustered, turning bright pink, but smiled broadly. "Th-thank you, sir."

"No need to thank me. Wasn't me who gave you your brains. Now, I need you to send another wire to Boston. Dead man is an associate of Brown. Name's George Roberts. And I'll need another sketch done. Storm's passed, so I'll be going up to Aurora tomorrow and I'd like to take a sketch of this Roberts fellow."

Hodgins stood and handed the reports back to Barnes. "Supposed to be my day off. If you find out anything important, you know where to find me. But *only* if it's something that can't wait until tomorrow."

CHAPTER FIFTEEN

Sweat dripped down Hodgins' back as he trudged through the deep snow. Not too many had ventured out that morning, except to go to church, so it hadn't been trampled down much. The snow crunched and squeaked under his boots and he cursed himself for not taking the trolley. He waved at Mr. Halloday, who stopped sweeping his walk when he spotted him. Hodgins hurried up his own walkway, not wanting to be delayed by his chatty neighbour.

The sounds of giggling children and Scraps' loud, deep bark came from the back of his house. With the children out of the way, he thought it would be the perfect opportunity to have anther talk with his brother.

After hanging his coat in the hallway, he looked in the sitting room for Jonathan, but it was empty. Pots and dishes rattled in the kitchen, so he followed the sound. He found Cordelia and Elizabeth chopping the vegetables for their evening meal.

"Ah, your tasty Irish stew. Can hardly wait." He

kissed his wife, then turned to Elizabeth. "Where might I find that brother of mine?"

"Out there." Elizabeth pointed at the window.

Hodgins peered over her shoulder and spotted Jonathan helping the children build a snow fort. Discussion pushed aside, he smiled. "Looks like fun. Think I'll join them."

* * *

Hodgins rose early and tried not to disturb his wife. He tip-toed to the window to see if any more snow fell overnight. The light from the gas streetlights cast a soft glow over the road, looking much the same as when he arrived home the previous evening. Hodgins jumped when a hand touched his shoulder.

"I didn't mean to startle you. Is something the matter?"

"No, Delia. Just checking the weather. Looks like a fine day for a train ride. I need to speak with Brown's widow again, and Jonathan, if I can get him alone. Somebody's not telling me everything."

"It's chilly. Come back to bed. It's too early to catch the train." Delia took his hand and gave it a gentle tug. "I think there's something you're not telling me. What is it? Is that second body connected to the first?"

"I can't sleep. Go back to bed. I'll tell you later."

"Why don't we chat over a cup of tea? I'll never get back to sleep now." She picked up their dressing gowns from the top of the chest at the foot of the bed and held out her arm. "Put this on Bertie. And don't forget your slippers."

Careful not to disturb anyone else in the house, Cordelia went into the kitchen and Hodgins started a fire in the sitting room. Cordelia joined him, carrying a tray with her Winter Rose teapot, two matching cups, and a plate of biscuits and cheese. She sat it on a small table beside one of the chairs and poured out the tea. Once they were settled, she inclined her head, indicating she was ready to listen. He let out a deep sigh and began.

"The second body was an associate of Brown's. And he had one of Jonathan's business cards in his pocket. Shot in the head, just like Brown. If Jonathan wasn't my brother…"

"But he's been here, with us. How could he have shot that man? And he wasn't even in Toronto when Brown was shot. Oh Bertie, you don't really believe he's involved, do you?"

He shrugged. "I don't know what to think. People change. I haven't seen him for over a decade. The policeman in me says he's high on my suspect list. He knows both men. He has a bad history with them. And I don't know for certain what happened between Jonathan and Janel Brown. If it was just a few comments, as he says, why such a change in her demeanor when she realized I'm his brother? That look on her face was pure hatred."

"Well, when put like that, it is suspicious." She thought for a moment. "I suppose he could have hired someone, or taken an earlier train."

He laughed. "That's my girl. Thinking like a detective."

Hodgins picked up one of the biscuits and a piece of cheese, but didn't put them in his mouth. "I hate to ask, but would you mind doing a bit of snooping for me?"

Cordelia's face lit up. "I'd love to help, you know that. You've never asked me to do anything before. Is it dangerous?"

He feigned shock. "Dangerous? You sound as though you welcome it. Are you that discontented?"

"Bertie, how can you suggest such a thing." Cordelia smiled. "It does become rather tedious at times, though. Cooking, cleaning, sewing. A change is most welcome. What sort of snooping would you like me to do?"

"When you're tidying up, would you mind going through Jonathan's things? Look for anything unusual. See if you can find his train ticket."

Delia clapped her hands. "Oh, how exciting. Now,

how will I get him out of the house?" She placed a finger on her chin and tilted her head, thinking. "Maybe I can ask him to take the children out to cut down a Christmas tree? I know you wanted to do that, though. Would you mind terribly?"

"No, that's a rather clever idea. I don't know when I'll have the time now, and the children were rather disappointed when I cancelled yesterday."

"I know I should feel horrible going through his things, but it's so exciting."

The clock in the hall struck seven. "Gracious, is that the time? Sara can stay home from school again today. Even though arrangements have been made for Cora and Freddy to attend with Sara until winter break, there's no need to send them off right away. They've only just arrived. And today would be a perfect time to cut down a tree."

"I'll stop at the school and let them know not to expect the children until tomorrow. Now, we'd best get dressed. It's going to be a busy day for everyone. Oh, and tell Jonathan to go where Father used to take us for our tree. Best spruce in the area. If you find anything of interest, be certain to bring it to the station immediately. I never thought I'd say this, but I hope to God I don't see you."

As they ascended the stairs, Hodgins asked what excuse she'd give for not going with them.

"It's almost Christmas Bertie. I'll simply tell them I need to wrap presents and don't want them spying."

* * *

Rather than going to his station house after stopping at Ketchum School, Hodgins walked further up Davenport to see if anyone was home at the previously empty house on Bishop. Unfortunately, whoever lived there still wasn't home. He went to the house next door to inquire about their neighbours on the corner, only to be told they'd moved a few weeks earlier.

CHAPTER SIXTEEN

It was almost 8:30 when Hodgins arrived at Station Four. The Northern Railway train to Aurora was scheduled to depart at 9:15. He went straight to Barnes' desk without bothering to remove his overcoat.

"Barnes, is there a copy of the morning paper about?"

"Yes, sir." Barnes didn't make any attempt to fetch it for him.

Everyone became quiet and stared at Hodgins. He held out his hand. "I'll read it on the train."

Barnes reached down and opened his desk drawer, then slowly pulled out the paper. "I'm sorry," he whispered as he handed it over.

Hodgins rolled up the newspaper and shoved it in the pocket of his overcoat before heading for Union Station. Fortunately, an empty cab approached so he hailed it, enjoying a surprisingly quick ride down to Simcoe Street. The train just pulled in as he arrived, leaving only a short time for him to purchase his return ticket and settle down. He chose a seat in the corner, hoping no one would join him. Curious as to the reaction back at the station, he pulled out the newspaper. The story was on the front page.

"Damn!"

The woman sitting across the isle gasped, then turned to face him. "Sir, there are ladies and children present. I would appreciate it if you'd watch your language."

"Terribly sorry, ma'am. I do apologize."

Slightly red-faced, both from embarrassment and the headline, he went back to the paper and re-read it.

DETECTIVE'S BROTHER WANTED FOR MURDER

Below was a less-than-flattering sketch of Hodgins. As he read through the half-truths, he noticed no source had been listed as to who gave the interview. He puzzled over how the reporter knew about Jonathan's involvement. He hadn't told anyone about the business cards even though they were mentioned in his station's report. Someone must have spoken to the reporter, but why? When he returned, he'd be sure to track down that reporter and provide the correct information. He continued reading.

> Highly regarded Toronto detective, Albert Hodgins of Station House Four on Wilton Avenue, has a murderer as a house-guest.

A string of obscenities flew from his mouth, a little louder than expected.

"Really, sir. I must insist you conduct yourself in a

better manner."

Once again, he apologized, then looked around the train at the other passengers. Beyond the glares of women with small children, he spotted several men at the opposite end of the rail car. He moved down, apologizing again as he passed the shocked women. He noticed a newspaper among the parcels one of the women had and hoped she hadn't read it and recognized him. He slipped into the seat behind the business men. They were discussing the lead story in the paper.

"Corrupt coppers, the lot of 'em. I'll wager a days pay that Hodgins fellow gets his brother off and frames some innocent chap."

"I don't know," a second one said. "I went to school with Jonathan. Wouldn't hurt a fly. You know as well as I do those reporters make up a lot of their stories."

Hodgins smiled, trying to place who the man was that knew his brother. He'd only glanced at them, but the one by the window seemed familiar.

"Think I'll look up Jonathan. Haven't spoken to him in years."

"Hmm… you may be right," the first man said. "But I do know for a fact some coppers ain't above a bribe or two. Did you know this Detective Hodgins fellow?"

"Not very well. He's a few years younger, but I can't

recall him ever getting into the same mischief as the rest of us."

Hodgins felt a little less angry, and hoped other people wouldn't believe the rot that was printed. Trying to push the story from his mind, he returned to the paper and read the rest of the news as the train pulled out of the station. The men in front of him changed the subject, talking instead of their day's business.

A little over an hour later the men left the train at the Richmond Hill stop and he got another glimpse of their faces, but still couldn't place the one who knew Jonathan. The rest of the ride to Aurora was uneventful and he exited the train forty minutes later. His first visit was to the Widow Brown. She was still rather hostile towards him upon opening her door.

"What is it Detective? I've only just buried my husband and I am rather busy." She held the door open only enough to talk to him. He wasn't sure if to keep the cold air out, to hide something, or simply dissuade him.

"Please, I only need a few minutes of your time."

She considered his request for a moment, then opened the door fully. "If you must." She stepped back to allow entry, indicating for him to go into the same room as before. A fire blazing in the stone fireplace, instantly warming him up. There were crates and trunks everywhere, except on the chairs. Rather than sitting, he stood by the fire.

"Moving?"

"Yes. There's nothing here for me now. I'm going back to Boston soon. What is it? I'm rather busy as you can see." She lowered herself onto one of the chairs, but remained perched at the edge.

"As I said, I'll only take a few minutes. It's about your friend, George Roberts."

She appeared surprised when his name was mentioned. "I wouldn't say he's a friend, exactly. What about him?"

"He's been murdered."

Janel didn't seem shocked by the news. "Oh, is that all? If the only reason for your visit was to tell me that, you've wasted a trip. It's no concern of mine."

"Yes, well, I was hoping you could tell me why he was here, in Toronto. Did he have business with your husband?"

"Yes, they were partners. Have been for years. Can't tell you what scheme they were planning. Something in the city."

That last comment confused Hodgins. "If they were planning something downtown, why live so far north? That just doesn't make any sense. A two-hour train ride isn't a very convenient get-a-way."

Janel gave the detective a look of disgust. "You didn't know my Tony. Despite his faults, he loved me and the children. We moved here because there's so much space. If we'd moved into Toronto we'd be crammed into a tiny flat. Probably dirty, too. We wanted to raise our children better than what we were."

He nodded. "You're right. I didn't know your husband at all. And I completely understand wanting to raise your children in a small town."

Hodgins had seen both the good and bad sides of Toronto. He shuttered at the thought of what his circumstance would be like if he hadn't come from a respectable, middle-class family. He couldn't imagine life without Cordelia and Sara. Janel cleared her throat, bringing Hodgins back to the present.

"Do you know of anyone here that your husband associated with? Any friends or maybe another partner in this scheme?"

He recalled the young man at Campbell's rope factory and how quickly he came up with the Brown's address. He flipped through his notebook to recall the name and see if Janel mentioned him. Before he could find him, she answered.

"Well, there was Ace. He came here a few times, but

Tony preferred to meet him elsewhere, usually at one of the hotels." Hodgins looked up from his notebook just in time to see the hint of a smile disappear from her lips.

A knock at the door interrupted their chat. She pushed herself and her unborn child off the high-back chair. Hodgins rushed over to assist, but she shook off his hand.

"I'm perfectly capable of getting up myself." She eased her child-laden body off the edge and pushed up on the arms of the chair.

He thought she was amazingly large for seven months and wondered if she might be carrying another set of twins. For her sake, he hoped not. The person at the front door knocked two more times before Janel managed to waddle the short distance.

Hodgins remembered when Delia carried Sara. Right up to the end she refused his help, despite the struggle to do the smallest thing and she hadn't been near as big. He imagined Brown had had his hands full with Janel. He could see a fair bit of his Delia in her. Must be part Irish. Janel returned with an elderly woman.

He helped the woman over to one of the chairs by the fire while Janel sat on the other, glaring at him. It was clear she didn't want him around any longer. He ignored her and introduced himself.

"Oh, a policeman. I do hope you catch the scoundrel who murdered poor Mr. Brown. Decent people aren't safe anywhere these days."

"We're doing all we can, ma'am." It seemed obvious to him that Mr. Brown's occupation wasn't well known. "Are you a relative?"

"No, just a neighbour. Poor girl needs someone to help now that's she's all alone." She looked around the room. "Are you moving my dear?"

Hodgins intended to inquire about her relationship with Jonathan, but he didn't want to raise the question in front of the neighbour. "I'll leave you to your visit. We'll let you know when we've made an arrest. Can you give me your new address?"

"Nothing's settled yet. I'll leave word at your station before I leave."

He excused himself and headed to the main core of Aurora, stopping at the hotel on the corner of Wellington and Yonge. It was almost across the road from Campbell's and probably a gathering place for the workers. He sat at one of the tables in the dining area. A server was at his side before he had time to remove his coat.

"Cottage Pie, if you have it, and a pot of tea."

He asked about Brown and Roberts, showing him the sketched of the two dead men, receiving only shrugs and vague answers. The staff admitted they'd been in a time or two, but claimed to know nothing of their business.

Once Hodgins' meal was finished, he walked down one side of Yonge Street, stopping at the various shops, inquiring about the two men, and someone called Ace. Hodgins continued to show the sketches of Brown and Roberts, but no one recognized either. He was relieved he didn't have to stop long at the blacksmith's as the sickly-sweet smell of seared hooves turned his stomach.

He got the same negative responses at each place of business. He crossed the road and turned back north, receiving the same reaction from each shop-keeper. One of the clerks at Doan's General Store recognized Janel Brown, but couldn't provide any information other than she was a regular customer and not terribly social. Frustrated, he continued up Yonge Street to Campbell's to have another chat with Wally. Maybe he knew who Ace was.

"Mr. Campbell, sorry to interrupt your day, but I'd like to speak with Wally again."

"Sorry, but he's sick. Damn fine time, too. He's the only one strong enough to make the ship ropes. Order's due next week. First time making ropes for ships and if I deliver on time, there could be more."

"Must be this cold weather. Few of my men are ill as

well."

As Hodgins turned to leave, Campbell grabbed his arm.

"You don't think Wally had anything to do with the murder you're looking into, do you? He seems to be a good lad. Strong, but not much brains. Wouldn't hurt anyone."

"No, but he knew the man and I hoped he could provide some information. I'll come back in a few days."

Frustrated and a little dejected, Hodgins made his way to the train station. He picked up a local paper to fill the hour before the next train was due. After arriving at the station, he sat on a bench near the wood burning stove and reviewed the meagre notes he'd accumulated, pondering over the notation that Wally had visited the Brown's home a few times. He was about the same age as Janel, at least ten years younger than Anthony Brown. He was also strong and rather good looking. Could Wally have paid visits when her husband was away? Had she been unfaithful? She'd been extremely angry at Jonathan's advances. Yes, he was older, but he'd always had girls vying for his attention at school. And he was a successful businessman. Had she rejected one man for another or was he reading too much into it? He'd gauge Wally's reactions when he got to speak with him. Maybe he'd at least know about Ace, and what his relationship to Janel Brown was.

Since Hodgins had little information to review, he put the notebook back in his overcoat pocket and opened the newspaper to see if the local news was any better than Toronto's. He found more talk of the compulsory voting bill, something also found in the Toronto paper. Hodgins smiled as he read the account of a speech made by the MP for North York on his recent visit to Aurora. Apparently, it didn't go well as the audience laughed at Mr. Dymond's comments. Hodgins laughed out loud when he spotted the notice for the County of York's coroner, Dr. Strange. He couldn't imagine anyone being stranger than his own Dr. Hamish McKenzie.

He left the paper on the bench when the train pulled in. The cars were almost empty so he had his pick of seats. Again, he moved to a back corner. When the train pulled into the Richmond Hill station the same men he'd overheard on the way up boarded. The one who knew Jonathan spotted him and came over.

"You're Jonathan's younger brother, Albert, I believe? The detective."

"Yes. You were one of Jonathan's classmates, but I'm afraid I don't recall your name."

"Eustace Billings."

"Ah, Billings. Your family owns one of the largest medical equipment suppliers in these parts."

"That's correct. And if today's business went as well as I think it did, we'll be number one in no time. Mind if we join you?"

Hodgins waved his hand towards the seats opposite. "By all means. I'm guessing these men are in business with you?"

"Where are my manners? May I present Timothy Grainger and David Perkins. My top salesmen. I've been trying to acquire a small company. Who better to sweet-talk the owner into selling than two such convincing salesmen?"

The three men laughed heartily and Hodgins smiled and nodded, figuring they were little better than con-men, or simply bullies. To Hodgins, they had the appearance of thugs rather than salesmen. Only Billings seemed comfortable in his suit, as the two salesmen continually tugged at their collars and loosened their ties.

Billings became serious and leaned towards Hodgins. "I read that ole Johnny has himself in a spot of bother. Nothing to it, I hope?"

"Newspaper reporters. You know what they're like." Hodgins had a vague recollection of a less than flattering story about the Billings Pharmaceuticals a while back. He raised an eyebrow and looked directly at Billings when he spoke. "Don't always get the facts straight, do they?"

Billings touched the side of his nose and winked. "Spot on there old chap. Twist the facts so much they're barely recognizable. I was saying to my associates just this morning there's no way Jonathan could be responsible for it. Why, I recall one time in school several of us were rough-housing and someone, don't recall who, ended up with a bloody nose. Jonathan damn near fainted." He paused and laughed. "If Johnny were to kill someone more likely than not, you'd find him passed out along side the corpse."

Hodgins remembered the two episodes in the coroner's office and almost blurted it out, but decided not to make his brother appear too weak to an old school mate. He simply agreed, and they all laughed at some length.

"At least he has an alibi for both murders," Hodgins remarked once they'd composed themselves.

"Both? You man there's been another?" Billings asked.

"Yes. I suppose the other hasn't made it to the papers, yet. Didn't see it in the morning edition. He was home with me when that one happened."

"And he was at the Red Lion when the first took

place."

That statement caught Hodgins off guard, but he managed to avoid appearing surprised. How many more things was Jonathan keeping from him? He didn't want to discuss it further so he changed the subject.

"Afraid I can't go into much detail about the case. You understand. Tell me, what have you been up to, besides the family business? Do you have a family of your own?"

Hodgins half-listened and politely smiled and nodded the rest of the way to Union Station. Between Billings and his two salesmen, Hodgins now knew more about medical supplies than he cared to. They parted with the promise of a visit from Billings before Jonathan returned to Boston.

Once Hodgins arrived home, he dragged his brother outside, barely giving him time to button his overcoat.

"Just when where you planning on telling me you arrived in Toronto before I met your train?" Hodgins took long strides as he walked along the street.

"Slow down. How did you find out?" Jonathan hurried to catch up to his brother.

"You grew up in Toronto and still have old friends here. You were seen. The Red Lion of all places. If you didn't want to be seen, why go to a public place? You have no alibi for Brown's murder now. Come to think of it, you don't really have one for Roberts' either. You could easily have snuck out of the house while we were asleep."

Jonathan grabbed his brother's arm and pulled him to a stop. "Albert, surely you don't believe I had anything to do with either man's death?"

"I don't know you any more. You've been in Boston for a long time and have some questionable associates. Your card was found on both bodies. If you were me, would you not think you guilty?"

Jonathan stared at him in disbelief, mouth open slightly. "I can see how it looks, but I haven't changed that much. I swear on my children's lives, it wasn't me."

He paused before answering, mulling everything over. Finally, he sighed and put a hand on Jonathan's shoulder. "I believe you, but not because you're my brother." He smiled. "As someone recently pointed out, with your constitution, we'd probably have found you passed out alongside the bodies. What say we go back home where it's warm?"

Once they settled in front of the fire Hodgins continued their earlier conversation.

"Someone must be framing you. You've been out of the city for a decade, so why would anyone here be murdering people and trying to blame you?"

Jonathan shrugged. "I can't recall anyone that I

angered ten years ago, at least not enough to murder innocent people over." He snickered. "Not that Brown or Roberts are exactly innocent of much."

"That's just it. The two murdered men are from Boston. It has to be connected to your business somehow. Could there be someone with a grudge against them who knows you've had a run in with them? Get rid of his enemies and blame someone else."

"Afraid I can't think of anyone. Wish I could."

Hodgins remembered his short conversation with Janel Brown. "Know a chap by the name of Ace?"

"Odd name. Can't say I've come across anybody that goes by it."

"Give it a think for a day or two." He rose from the chair. "Smells like it's about time to eat."

CHAPTER SEVENTEEN

Excitement grew as the time to erect the Christmas tree neared. Even though many people with children waited until the little ones had gone to bed Christmas Eve to put up the tree, Hodgins preferred to enjoy it earlier. Both Cordelia and Sara agreed. Without being asked, Sara, Cora, and Freddie cleared up after dinner and even washed the dishes. Hodgins and his brother went out back to where the tree leaned against the house.

Albert grabbed the tree with one hand and stood it upright for a better look. "Red Spruce, just like when we were children. One of my favourites. Father's too."

"It is a nice tree. Not many left though. Shame. Is there another area where they grow?"

"Not that I've found. Maybe farther north. Now help me get this thing into the porch so I can nail the boards to the bottom."

After about a quarter hour, the tree stood in front of the bay window in the sitting room.

"Little shaky, isn't it?" Jonathan observed.

"Got that covered. Check the edge of the inside sill."

Jonathan peered behind the tree and tried to see what his brother was talking about. "All I see is a nail."

"Watch and learn, big brother." Hodgins pulled a length of string from his pocket, put a slip knot in one end and tightened it over a nail in the sill on one side of the tree. Then, he wrapped the string around the trunk, then fastened it to a nail on the other side.

"If it falls, it won't go far. It's the first tree with the dog and I don't know if he'll leave it alone."

"Brilliant idea. I'll have to try that myself next Christmas. Freddie managed to knock it over once last year."

"May we decorate now, Daddy?" Sara and her cousins stood behind them, holding the paper chains they'd been making.

"Yes, you may." He stood aside as the children rushed to the tree.

"It's larger than last year's." Cordelia and Elizabeth stood in the doorway. "At least a foot taller. I'm not sure our star will fit on the top," Cordelia said.

"Too late to cut it shorter now. If it doesn't fit it'll just have to sit near the top. A bit of string will hold it in place. Got plenty." Hodgins patted his pocket.

"Do you have any store-bought ornaments?"

Elizabeth asked.

"Yes, but I'm afraid to put them on just yet. Look how Scraps is sniffing around the tree. He might break them. I think I'll wait until Christmas Eve and put them on before lighting the candles." Cordelia turned to her husband. "Bertie, can you help me get them down from the attic?"

Hodgins knew Cordelia had put them away herself and didn't require his assistance, but she winked, indicating she wanted to get him out of earshot. She waited until they were in the attic before she spoke.

"I went through Jonathan's things, but I'm afraid I didn't find his train ticket. I did find this, however."

She reached into the pocket of the apron she still had tied around her waist and handed him a folded napkin. He opened it and saw it had the emblem for the Red Lion, along with writing. Jonathan's barely legible handwriting. He could only make out a few words: Aurora, Brown, and Roberts.

"One of the words may be Inn, but I can't make out which inn. And here, it says twelfth or possibly thirteenth. That coincides with Roberts' murder."

"But when was he at the Red Lion?" Cordelia asked.

He looked up at her. "I'll tell you about that later. I don't suppose you discovered this someplace where it would have easily been found cleaning?"

"No, it was in a pocket."

"It's already come out that he was at the Red Lion. But if Jonathan isn't forthcoming with any more details, I'll have to figure out a way to let him know we have the napkin, as I may have to put it with the other evidence. Things have a habit of falling out of pockets. I can say you found it on the floor while cleaning. Now, where are those ornaments we came up here for? They'll come looking for us if we don't go back down soon."

* * *

The Chief Inspector had been out of town, so the Inspector hadn't been badgering Hodgins for any further updates. Out of courtesy, Hodgins let the Inspector know what his plans were, and promised another update before the Chief returned. Hodgins waited a couple of days before taking the train back up to Aurora. The constables that had been off nursing their sour stomachs had finally returned to duty, so he hoped Wally suffered from the same illness and might have returned to the rope factory. Unfortunately, he was still off.

"Damn inconsiderate of him to be sick." Campbell paced across his tiny office. "That big order for the shipping company needs to be sent soon. If Wally isn't back right quick it won't be ready. I pride myself on always delivering on time. Not easy to find someone with the muscles to turn the larger ropes. Maybe it's time to convert to steam power. At least those blasted machines don't bugger off."

Hodgins pulled a card from his pocket and handled it to Campbell. "Let me know when he's back."

Campbell took the card and tossed it on his paper-covered desk. "You don't believe Wally had anything to do with this other dead man, do you?"

"Just want to ask him a few questions. He knew Brown, so maybe he also knows Roberts. I'm hoping he can tell me more about them."

Hodgins remembered the sketch of George Roberts he had done up and took it out of his overcoat pocket.

"Ever seen this man around?"

Campbell examined the sketch before handing it back. "Sorry. Doesn't look familiar."

Hodgins left the ropemakers factory, not certain where to go next. If Brown and Roberts both worked as labourers for Jonathan, maybe one of them had found employment somewhere in town. As he had no idea where anything was, he listened for any sounds that might direct him. He heard a fair bit of racket off to the west, so he walked down to Wellington Street and turned right. He discovered not one, but two, plow makers. He stopped first at Wilkinson's as it was on the same side of the street. No one there admitted to knowing Brown, Roberts, or Ace, so he crossed to the south side and entered the Fleury Works.

He discovered both Brown and Roberts worked there briefly, but had been fired. Unlike at Jonathan's business, they hadn't been let go due to theft, but rather for incompetence. Somehow, the two men had managed to render a large quantity of plows useless.

The foreman clenched both hands at the mention of the two men. "Fell apart right in the foundry. Can you imagine if that had happened after shipping? They were due to go out west that day. No one would've ever bought from us again. What have they done now? Ruined someone's business I suspect."

"No. They've managed to get themselves murdered."

The foreman laughed. "When you find the chap what done them in, let me know. I'd like to buy him a drink."

Hodgins smiled. "I think you might have to wait in line for that honour. Don't suppose you know anyone who goes by the name of Ace?"

The foreman shook his head, but a nearby worker butted in. "I think I might know who you mean. Fellow over at Campbell's goes by Ace."

Hodgins cursed and thanked both men, then turned

back to Campbell's. He stopped the first employee he encountered.

"Where can I find Ace?"

"Off sick."

Hodgins spotted Campbell towards the back of the long building and yelled to get his attention. The two men met mid-way down the building.

"I understand you employ someone who goes by Ace."

Campbell looked surprised. "Why, that's Wally. Already told you he's still off."

Hodgins berated himself for not asking about him earlier. "Why is he called Ace?"

"Full name's Wallace. Ace for short.

"Wally. Wallace. I should have figured that out myself." This business with Jonathan must have him more rattled than he realized. Was it a coincidence that Wally, Ace, was sick at this particular time? Hodgins remembered the half-smile from Janel Brown.

"Tell me, when exactly did Wally become ill?"

Campbell thought for a moment. "Why, right after your first visit. He finished the day, but hasn't been in since." He wrung his hands. "You don't think...?"

Hodgins nodded. "Yes, I'm beginning to believe he's somehow involved. I don't suppose you can vouch for his whereabouts the evening of December 4? It was a Friday."

Campbell smiled. "Yes, I can actually. I treated my workers to a night out for all their hard work this year. Sort of a Christmas party, at the hotel on the corner, the Queen's."

Hodgins pulled out his notebook and started writing. "Are you absolutely positive he was in attendance the entire evening?" He made a note to check the train schedule. Two hours down, murder someone and two hours back. Longer if he went by horse. He already knew the answer before Campbell spoke.

"It's a long trip down to Toronto. I'd have noticed such a lengthy absence."

Hodgins closed the little black book. "Yes, I totally agree. Maybe it is nothing more than a coincidence. I'd like to check on him myself through. Could you give me his address?"

Hodgins followed Campbell to his office and waited while he wrote out the address and provided directions. Wally lived on Tyler Street, right at the corner of Tyler and George Streets. It didn't take long to walk there.

No one answered his knock. He tried several times, but the only sound was the brass knocker against the thick oak door. Hodgins walked around, peering in each of the windows. He didn't spot anyone in any of the rooms on the ground floor. He was looking in a window at the back of the house when a hand touched his shoulder. He jumped, knocking his head against the glass.

CHAPTER EIGHTEEN

An elderly gentleman stood behind Hodgins, chuckling as Hodgins rubbed his head. "May I help you, young man?"

Hodgins showed his badge. "Looking for Wally. He's not been at work for a while. Are you his neighbour?"

"Bin living next door for 'bout ten years. Seen my fair share of folk coming and going from this house. 'Fraid you've missed the young buck. Headed out with a large trunk, oh, two, maybe three days ago."

"Don't suppose he said where he was going?"

"Only saw 'im through the winder. Why don't you come inside out of the cold and have a proper chat. Wife's just made a batch of oatmeal cookies. Tell you everything I know about young Wally Caster."

Both Mr. Gardiner and his wife knew quite a bit about Wally, most simply gossip. The one interesting tid-bit was the fact that Wally originally came from Boston and spoke about going back soon. He hadn't been in town more than four months. Could he have gone back to the

States? The puzzle pieces started to come together, but a large gap still needed to be filled in. Two cups of tea and three cookies later, Hodgins headed back to the train station.

* * *

Before going home, Hodgins made his way to Station House Four up on Wilton. He left instructions not to be disturbed, then transcribed his notes onto several sheets of long paper. It was late when he arrived back home and the children were all in a bed. Cordelia cut two thick slices of bread and several pieces of the roast she'd warmed for dinner. She'd managed to stretch it out longer then anticipated.

Jonathan sat in the sitting room reading the newspaper, Elizabeth in a chair beside a small table containing a hurricane lamp. She'd moved it to the edge to better catch the light, the candle inside illuminating the needlework she'd brought with her. Cordelia left them alone and stayed in the kitchen with her husband while he ate.

"There are so many seemingly connected pieces of information that just don't completely fit together. It's so frustrating." He took another bite of his beef sandwich then washed it down with a sip of tea.

"Tell me what you know so far." Cordelia poured

herself some tea. "Maybe you'll discover something as you speak."

"Well, as you know, my dear brother is at the top of my list, even though I truly believe him innocent. He knew both victims and did have problems with them in the past. Then, there's the two tramps, but we have witnesses to confirm where they were at the time of Brown's murder. Can't connect them to Roberts' as they're still in Berlin, and at the Sheriff's. Can't have a better alibi than that."

He rose and went over to the wood stove and cut a piece from the apple pie that sat on top, still warm.

"Funny thing. Brown's wife is packing up, planning on returning to Boston and someone I spoke to about Brown up in Aurora has disappeared. Seems he's also from Boston."

"You don't think there's something between this man and the Widow Brown, do you?"

"I must admit it crossed my mind. She's a beautiful young woman and the missing man, Wally Caster, is young, strong and quite handsome. He was at a party when Brown was killed, though. The only person whose whereabouts can't be confirmed is Jonathan."

"Don't be ridiculous. Jonathan was on a train when Mr. Brown was killed, and right here in our own home for the second murder."

Hodgins swirled around the remnants of his tea. "Found out the other day Jonathan actually came into the city Thursday night. That's why he had the napkin from the Red Lion. Never had a chance to tell you. As for George Roberts, Jonathan could have snuck out while we were sleeping."

Cordelia gasped. "Oh Bertie, how can you think such a thing?"

"I don't believe it, but others will. I'm missing something and if I don't figure out what, Jonathan may very well hang.

* * *

When Hodgins arrived at the station the next morning he had a wire sent to Boston inquiring about Wallace Caster, then made a cup of tea and shut himself away in his office to think. "Who could have killed both men and why were they framing Jonathan?" He mumbled to himself. "Whoever it was, was doing a damn fine job of making Jonathan appear guilty. How could anyone know when he wouldn't have an alibi? It has to be someone nearby."

He tore a clean sheet off his pad of long paper, listing the people he needed to follow-up with, or make further inquires about.

At the top he wrote down the two tramps, Curly and Scotty. Beside their names he indicated that he'd confirmed their whereabouts.

Next, Jonathan. Hodgins tapped his pencil while thinking. What could he write that had been absolutely confirmed? He started jotting points.

Arrived mid-night Friday – No

Red Lion early Friday evening – confirmed

Opportunity to kill Brown? – probably not

At home when Roberts was killed? – unknown

He moved on to Ace/Wally

Opportunity to kill Brown? – No

Whereabouts when Roberts was killed? – unknown

Relationship to Janel Brown? – unknown

Hodgins couldn't think of anyone else to add to his list. He re-read it and put little stars beside Ace/Wally. So far, he hadn't found out much about him. Another visit to Aurora was needed. But first, he had to set that reporter straight and provide the public with the facts, such as they were.

He started to put on his coat when the inspector opened the door, slamming it behind him. The glass rattled in the frame. The inspector had Monday's paper in his hand, and threw it on Hodgins' desk.

The tick over the inspector's right eye told Hodgins he wasn't simply angry, he was mad as hell, and that was never good. "Just now finding time to catch up on the paper and saw this. Why isn't he in jail?" The inspector jabbed his finger over the interview on the front page. "Who the hell spoke to the reporter anyway?"

"I don't know, and Jonathan's not guilty. I picked him up at Union Station myself at almost midnight the day of the murder, and he was at my home when the second occurred." He stood with his hands clasped behind his back, fingers crossed. He hadn't lied, just omitted a few details.

The inspector jabbed at the newspaper again. "Fix this. Now."

"Yes, sir. I fully intend to track down that reporter and correct the interview. Someone is framing him and I intend to find out who and why."

The inspector harrumphed. The tick over his eye slowed, and Hodgins relaxed, a little. "See that you do, else you may just find yourself reporting to Barnes." He turned, yanking the door open, letting it bang against the wall. Hodgins watched the door swing back, too stunned to grab it before it slammed shut.

Barnes knocked on the door and entered without waiting for a reply. "What's got the inspector in such a state? Haven't seen him that angry since… well, never."

Hodgins leaned back against his desk. "Bugger wants me to arrest my brother. If I don't arrest someone soon, he threatened to bust me lower than you."

"But I'm the lowest rank, sir."

"I know. Now, I need to you do something." Hodgins reached into his pocket for his notebook. "Go back to Davenport and speak with the folks around the school again. Maybe they've remembered something new. I need to go see that damn reporter."

Hodgins walked over to Yonge Street, took the trolley down to King Street, and then walked east. The newspaper office was at number twenty-six. Fortunately he'd recognized the reporter's name. Chatwick. Always hanging around the stations across the city looking for a scoop. Hodgins stormed into the newspaper office, but most of the desks were empty. He waited a quarter of an hour, pacing and fuming, until Chatwick finally appeared.

"Detective Hodgins. So glad you're here. Was just about to track you down. Hoping to interview you about these murders. Find out how you feel, what with your brother being a murderer and all."

Hodgins thrust the newspaper at Chatwick. "This is a load of shit and you know it. I expect the next edition will have a full retraction, complete with the *facts*, not that rot you printed Monday."

Chatwick shrugged. "Only printed what I was told. How would I know it wasn't the truth?"

"Next time you have a story that involves me or any of the men at Station Four, you talk to me before you print it. Unless you don't want anything from us in future. Imagine, no more police reports from my turf. Hmm, that might make us look rather good. No crime in my area at all."

Hodgins smiled at the expression on the reporter's face as it changed from smug to shock.

"Then again, if you'd like an exclusive when we find the man responsible…?"

"An exclusive?" Chatwick motioned Hodgins to an empty desk. "Tell me what you'd like me to print. It'll be in the evening edition."

Chatwick opened the desk drawer and pulled out several pieces of clean white paper. He stacked them neatly beside something shrouded with a cloth. Chatwick removed the cloth and tossed it behind his shiny, new Remington typewriting machine.

"I wish we had one of those contraptions at the station," Hodgins said. "Make the paperwork at least tolerable." He looked around and noticed several desks had a covered machine sitting on them.

Chatwick barely acknowledged Hodgins' comment. Instead, he picked up a single sheet and wove it through the roller. "Ok, shoot." His hands hovered over the keyboard waiting for Hodgins to start.

Hodgins told him about Jonathan's arrival, stressing his innocence, all the while staring in amazement as Chatwick picked away with two fingers. "Damn noisy thing."

"You get used to it. Maybe one day every office will have typewriting machines."

"City's too cheap," Hodgins remarked.

After correcting all the lies and half-truths, Hodgins went back home to talk to his brother. He didn't want Cordelia or Elizabeth to overhear his questions so he rushed Jonathan into a hansom and went west to The Miller Tavern. Fortunately, it wasn't busy. They found a quiet table in the corner and ordered two beers.

"It's time you told me everything. The inspector expects me to arrest you, and frankly, I don't blame him. I need to know about every incident that took place in Boston, no matter how trivial."

Jonathan shrugged. "I don't know what else to tell you."

"This is becoming tiresome. There has to be something. I won't judge you, but I need to know. Somebody's killed two men and is trying to have you hung for it. Why?"

Silence.

Hodgins slammed both hands on the table top, causing Jonathan to jump, and several nearby conversations to stop. "You know it takes very little to try my patience. Do you want me to put you in jail? The inspector would love that."

"No. Dear God, no." Jonathan picked up his beer, downed it, then signaled for another. The server nodded, stopping to clear several tables as she made her way to the bar. She returned with his beer, spilling a little when she placed it down. One quick swipe with a dirty rag and she was off to the next table. Jonathan finished the second before continuing.

"There's a reason I didn't check on Brown before hiring him and his friends. Some of my dealing have been... slightly around the law."

"How slightly? Am I going to have to let the authorities in Boston know?"

"Nothing too serious. I may have forgotten to list the occasional item on shipments going in and out of my warehouse."

"And I suppose it also slipped your mind when the taxes were collected?"

"It's possible."

"What else? I can't see anyone murdering people over that."

"I owe people money. The wrong kind of people, if you know what I mean. A lot of money. They probably think I've done a runner and may come looking for me."

Hodgins opened his notebook. "Give me their names and I'll see what I can find. If the Boston Police are interested in them, you may have to testify, so you might want to let Elizabeth know."

"She's not like your wife, Albert. I don't believe she'll take the news well."

"Would you prefer she found out as you were being dragged out of the house, in front of the children? I strongly suggest you sit her down and tell her everything."

Jonathan buried his head in his hands. His voice was muffled, but Hodgins understood his words. "I've been so stupid. Tell me what to do and I'll do it."

CHAPTER NINETEEN

Jonathan sat in front of his brother's desk at Station House Number Four, waiting for Albert to return with the promised coffee. Word had been left not to disturb them. Hodgins paused as soon as he came out of the back room. He could see Jonathan slouched in the chair, elbows on his knees, hands cradling his head. That wasn't the strong, over-confident big brother that moved to Boston with his new bride all those years ago. The man sitting in that chair was practically a stranger, and up to his neck in trouble. Hodgins went into his office with two cups and the entire pot of coffee. The inspector walked by and nodded when he spotted Jonathan.

"Right. First, you're going to tell me every sordid detail. This will be an official report so no half-truths or omissions. Then, you're going home to tell Elizabeth. You'll have to come up with something to tell the children, too. They may not read the newspaper, but the other children will hear their parents talking. Unless you intend to keep Freddie and Cora locked up inside until you return home to Boston, they'll need to be prepared. Understand?"

Jonathan nodded, poured some coffee into one of the cups, then began. Almost two hours passed by the time he stopped. Hodgins had several pages full of names, dates, and shipments.

Hodgins sat back and flexed his sore fingers. "You realize you could see a lot of jail time for this? Unless…"

Jonathan leaned forward. "Unless?"

"I wired those names you gave me earlier to the Boston Police. I'll include the new ones you just provided. If they express interest in them, maybe we can make a deal. You would have to testify in court back home and it'll do irreparable damage to your reputation and business."

"I'd have to move and start over. I don't know if I can do that."

"Once word gets out, and it will, you'll probably have to move anyway. No point in dwelling on it until we hear back from the authorities. They may have little interest in it."

"They'll be interested. The authorities have been after these people for a couple of years. I'll do whatever I have to. Moving is a better option than hanging. If they'll make a deal, I'll testify. It could get ugly."

Hodgins checked the time. "The children won't be

home from Sara's friends for a bit. Go home and tell Elizabeth. Maybe include Delia too. She's level-headed and will help calm Elizabeth. She can also help figure out what to tell the children. I'll take Delia and Sara over to the in-laws after dinner so you can have the house to yourselves to tell the little ones. Freddie may not understand, but Cora's bound be to quite upset."

Jonathan took a deep breath and ran his fingers through his hair. "You're right. I'll do it now. I'll fill Cordelia in, even though I suspect you've already told her most of it. Then the three of us can sit and discuss it." Jonathan stood, slipped into his overcoat, pulled his shoulders back, then walked confidently out the door.

* * *

Hodgins glanced at the somber faces around the breakfast table. Now that Jonathan's shady business dealings were out in the open, everyone seemed afraid to speak. Cora's eyes were red and swollen. Not a surprise as he'd heard her crying during the night. Sara fidgeted, unsure what to do or say. They'd told her about Jonathan's troubles on the way home from Cordelia's parents. Only Freddie seemed unaffected.

Cordelia tried to make breakfast as cheery as possible, softly singing a familiar Irish tune. Despite hard feelings between Hodgins and Delia's mother, Euphemia, he always admired her beautiful singing voice. Along with her red hair and freckles, Cordelia inherited that same voice from her mother. Hodgins caught her attention and shook his head. Delia acknowledged him with a nod and stopped singing before putting the breakfast on the table.

"Jonathan, as soon as I hear back from the Boston Police I'll send for you. Won't be able to decide on the best thing to do until we know more."

Cora burst into tears again and ran from the table, knocking the chair over. Scraps barked, then trotted after her. Sobs drifted into the kitchen from the sitting room. Freddie started crying and ran towards the front of the house to join her. Elizabeth rose, but Jonathan put his hand on her arm.

"I'll go. It's my mess. I'll try to explain it again. No matter what the outcome, there'll be no more side deals. I promise."

After he left, Elizabeth pushed her pancakes around the plate. Without looking up, she asked, "What's really going to happen to him?"

Her words sounded flat. Hodgins was unable to tell if she was upset or fed up. Were they headed towards another separation? Or something more final?

"I honestly don't know what will happen. As I said, we need to know what the authorities in Boston want.

Whatever the outcome, it won't bode well for his business. It's certain to be in the papers both here and in Boston. The only people who would want to deal with him would be criminals. However, if he testifies, even the crooks won't bother with him." Hodgins omitted the reminder Jonathan was still a suspect in two murders.

"His business will be ruined. None of our friends will ever speak to us again. We'll have to move."

"Why not move here?" Delia suggested. "Jonathan can stay in the import/export business. Toronto Harbour is just as busy a port as Boston."

"Oh, that would be wonderful," Sara said. "Cora is so nice. Please Aunt Elizabeth?"

"We'll see dear. There's much to discuss." Elizabeth pushed her plate away. "Excuse me. I need to check on the children."

"Well that was a pleasant meal." Hodgins popped the last bite of biscuit in his mouth, then finished his tea. "I need to get to the station." He kissed Delia and Sara before leaving.

As he put on his overcoat, he watched his brother and family in the sitting room. Freddie sat in front of the fireplace with Scraps, Elizabeth on the settee, Cora's head resting on her mother's shoulder. Jonathan stood staring out the bay window.

* * *

One of the sergeants brought a wire to Hodgins about an hour after he arrived. "Boston Police, sir."

Hodgins read the wire, then called Barnes in. "Fetch my brother, will you? Don't bother with the trolley, grab a hansom. Sharpish."

"Right away. Is something wrong?"

Hodgins smiled. "Not at all. Good news for a change. Now off with you."

Three quarters of an hour later, Jonathan raced into his brother's office. "Albert, what is it? Barnes said it was good news."

Hodgins waved the wire. "Boston authorities. As I suspected, they only want the men at the top. If you co-operate, they won't press any charges against you. I'd advise you pay the back taxes you omitted."

"That's a relief, but what about those two bodies? I won't go to jail for smuggling, but I may still be dancing on the end of a rope." Jonathan leaned forward. "You have to find the person responsible. I swear I didn't kill anyone."

"Can you give me any names to confirm your whereabouts Thursday, December 3? You were seen at the Red Lion. It's only a few blocks from where Brown's body was found, so you need to account for every second, from the time you arrived Thursday night, right through until I met you at the train station. How long were you there? Where were you before I met you at the station Friday evening?"

"You know I came in a week before my family to do business. That's what my meeting at the Red Lion was. I just came in a day earlier than I told you." Jonathan provided the names and addresses of the two men. "They cancelled after that story in the newspaper. I stayed overnight Thursday at the Red Lion. Staff there can vouch for me. My meeting was at five Friday evening. Had to come in Thursday as I couldn't catch the train that arrived Friday afternoon. Spent the entire day at the Red Lion, reading, chatting with the owner and staff. The meeting took longer than expected and I barely made it to the station before you arrived to pick me up."

"And I'll swear you never left my house when Roberts' was killed. Even if you by-passed the squeaky step, Scraps would have made a fuss and woke everyone. I'll send Barnes over to the Red Lion for statements."

Jonathan leaned back and grinned. "Well, I've nothing to worry about then, do I?"

"I'm confident saying you won't hang, but someone is framing you, and doing a damn fine job of it. If he doesn't succeed in getting you convicted, what else will he do? He might make it more personal. Could come after you."

"Or my family? Please, don't mention that to Lizzie. She's upset enough. She was even blathering on about moving here."

"Been meaning to talk to you about that. Delia mentioned it at breakfast and Sara got all excited about it. You already know once word gets out about your shady dealings your business will suffer. Would you consider moving back here?"

"I don't know. Maybe. Not a priority at the moment."

"Of course not. Think about it though. Now, shall I wire Boston and tell them you'll work with them when you arrive back home?"

Jonathan sighed. "Yes, I suppose you'd better. After the beginning of the year. Anything else?"

"No. Send Barnes in on your way out."

* * *

Barnes returned a few hours later with statements from the staff as well as from the owner of the Red Lion.

"Quite an interesting place. First time I've been in. About what I expected. Could use a better decorator, though. Place is littered with anvils, jackplanes, and even an old beer barrel. Why, they've even got a sheep's head mounted over the brick fireplace. Only nice thing was the dog." He pulled out his notebook and told Hodgins what he'd found.

"I spoke with several of the employees and they all recall seeing your brother drinking with two other chaps. One woman," Barnes flipped through his notes. "Sally, said he was there when she came on shift at six p.m." Barnes looked up at Hodgins and smiled. "The barman can't say one way or another when Jonathan left, but all the ladies remembered him."

Hodgins nodded. "Yes, he's always been popular with the women. Fortunately, he never took advantage of it." His thoughts drifted to the Widow Brown. "At least as far as I know."

"He came in late Thursday and spent the night. Owner said Jonathan stayed there all day Friday chatting to the staff, settling into the dining room around 5:30. Two men joined him for a meal and they stayed until about 10:30."

"Not proof positive he's not guilty, but it's enough to cast doubt. So, who are we left with?"

Barnes shrugged and shook his head. "No one we know of. Maybe someone involved in this deal of Brown's?"

"Problem is, the only person I know of is Roberts, and he's dead too. Mrs. Brown said she knows nothing of the business, but she could be lying. I got the impression she wasn't totally heart-broken over his death, and she seemed fed-up with his dealings. Before I informed her of his death, her response was a somewhat frustrated 'what has he done now?' or something similar."

Hodgins leaned back in his chair and twisted the end of his moustache. "I wonder…"

"Sir?"

"I need to mull a few things over. It's getting late. We'll continue this in the morning."

Hodgins rose and removed his overcoat from the peg. "Write up a report and get proper statements signed by the staff at the Red Lion. We'll need them if Jonathan goes to trial. Say, have you given any thought to coming over one night with your sweetheart? I think we all need a good old knees-up to brighten everyone's spirits. We're both scheduled the day off on Christmas Eve. Bring your family and hers. Delia and Elizabeth can put out a spread of cold meats and sweets. Who knows? Maybe we'll have something to celebrate by then."

CHAPTER TWENTY

Hodgins and Cordelia took a advantage of an unusually quiet house, relaxing in the two stuffed chairs by the fireplace. "A Christmas Eve party? That's sounds perfect. All our families together." Hodgins watched as Cordelia muttered and counted on her fingers. "Mother and Father can come in the afternoon, or before luncheon. Between Elizabeth, Mother and myself we can have everything ready by the time Henry and his family arrive. I assume the Halloway's will be coming, too? Can't have Henry without his sweetheart and her family." She stopped and wagged a finger in his face. "There will be no talk of Jonathan's connection to the two men."

Hodgins put his hands up. "I promise, I won't mention it. Only jolly discussions. Speaking of my brother, where is he?"

"Oh, an old friend dropped by and they went out to dinner. Billings I believe he said."

"Ran into him on the train the other day. Said he'd stop in to see Jonathan. If what he said on the train is true, at least Jonathan has one person on his side who's not related."

"Sit down and have some tea." Cordelia placed two cups on the kitchen table and filled them. "Dinner's almost ready, and the house is quiet for a change."

He sat beside his wife and took a sip of hot tea. "I thought there was something different. Where's Elizabeth and the children?"

"She took them skating."

Hodgins looked around. "Scraps too?"

"Yes. It's such a nice day they decided to go to the pond instead of the rink. That way Scraps could join them. I expect they'll be returning soon. I've gotten ever so much done this afternoon." She turned slightly to face him. "Are you any closer to finding out who murdered those two men?"

"No, but we found several witnesses to vouch for Jonathan's whereabouts for Brown's murder, and I'll swear six ways to Sunday he never left this house at the time of the second one. I'm confident we've enough to keep him out of jail and away from the noose."

Hodgins reached across the table and took a biscuit from the covered basket before Delia could slap his hand away. "Bertie, you really must stop eating so much. I don't think I can let your trousers out any further."

"I'll walk Scraps more often. It's worth it." He broke off a large piece of the biscuit and stuffed it in his mouth. "There's something different tasting about this."

"A recipe of Elizabeth's. Do you like it?"

"Not a good as yours but a delightful change." He ate another piece before continuing. "I'll be taking the first train back to Aurora tomorrow. I'm certain Brown's widow knows something, or that Wally bloke. She's packing up and he's already scarpered. I'd like to get this settled before Christmas, or at least by the end of the year. Jonathan has to go home right after the new year and testify. I don't want this hanging over his head. Even proven not guilty, word's bound to get out. I really hope he decides to move and put as much distance as possible between himself and the men he was dealing with.

* * *

It was going on eleven the next morning when Hodgins arrived back at the Brown residence. The coat pegs inside the door were empty, and the knick-knacks on the hall table were gone. He looked down the hall past Janel. The pictures were gone, too. She indicated for him to go into the sitting room where they spoke previously. Almost everything had been packed up. "Moving so soon?"

"I'm leaving tomorrow. I do wish you'd stop bothering me. There's nothing more I can tell you.

Hodgins leaned on the fireplace mantle. "Oh, I believe there's plenty you can tell me. You mentioned Ace last time I visited. That's young Wally Caster. Funny thing, he up and left town without a word. Headed back to Boston I believe." Hodgins only guessed at that, hoping Janel would say something to confirm it.

He reached over and read the tag on the nearest crate. "Same place your belonging are headed. Just how well do you know Wally?"

Janel placed her hand on her growing bulge. "What are you implying?"

Hodgins feigned surprise. "Why nothing at all ma'am. I was just making a casual obser—" He stopped, cocked his head, and starred off to the left, trying to recall something.

"Am I correct in remembering you said you're seven months along?"

"Yes, that's right."

"We received a rather lengthy report from the Boston Police. Listed many of your husband's stays in their jail. His most recent incarceration lasted only a few months. He was released mid-July, only five months ago."

"You're quicker than Tony. Took him two months to figure out the dates."

"Did he find out who fathered the child? Confront the man and end up dead, perhaps?"

Janel laughed. "No he was too stupid to see what was right under his nose."

Once again, her earlier half-smile popped into his mind. "Wally."

"Very good, Detective."

"But he didn't kill your husband. I know that for a fact."

Janel turned and casually strolled over to an end table with a single drawer, half-hidden by a doily. Hodgins heard the drawer slide open, then close. When she turned back towards him, a small Derringer was in her hand, pointed straight at his chest.

He held up his hands. "Hold on. I'm not going to arrest you for having another man's baby. Please, put the pistol down."

"I know you're an intelligent man, Detective. Surely you must have figured it out. Why else would you come here?"

He took one step closer. "I know you couldn't have killed anyone. Woman your size and condition would never have been able to drag a dead body into those positions. And your husband was dragged a fair distance. I'm sure if I asked around I'd find people to confirm Wally was here in town when Roberts was killed as well. Again, I'm asking you to put the gun down." He took another step.

Janel raised her arm, pointing the gun at his head. "Stay put. I need to think."

Hodgins gambled on his instincts. "Who'd you hire?"

She smiled. " See? I said you were intelligent. Tell me, do you treat your wife with respect? I image you do. Not like Tony. He treated me as a maid and housekeeper. Said I was too stupid to understand any of his plans. Well I showed him. I planned this." She waved her arms around. "All this was my idea. I wanted to start a new life with Ace, Wally. He's young, attractive and honest. Everything Tony wasn't."

"Does Wally even know it was you who arranged all these killings?"

"No." It was barely more than a whisper. Did she regret what she'd done, or did she think Wally would leave her if he found out? She lowered her arm, gun pointing at the floor. Hodgins took another step.

"But why kill Roberts? Surely you could have gone away and not killed him?"

"Your brother insulted me. Treated me like one of those trollops. Word got around he was planning a trip to Toronto to visit his brother, so I convinced Tony it would be a good idea to move here. So many more people to fleece. First, Ace moved and found a job. Tony had business cards from when he worked for your brother, so I made certain to take them. After we moved, I accompanied Tony into the city one day. While he made arrangements with Roberts I went shopping. Shopping for a hired killer. It wasn't difficult to find someone to kill both and leave the business cards. My revenge against your brother for treating me like a common tart."

She stopped pacing and pointed the gun again. "Unfortunately, it seems like I'll have to take care of you myself."

The safety release clicked. Hodgins flinched. He was too far from any of the piles of boxes and crates to dash behind. His gaze fixed on her hand. It started to shake. He held his breath, waiting for the shot.

CHAPTER TWENTY-ONE

One of the babies cried causing Janel to turn towards the hallway. Hodgins made his move. Three long strides and his hand clamped over her wrist.

"No!" Janel screamed. Hodgins squeezed her wrist, forcing her to drop the pistol.

"Afraid you won't be meeting Wally any time soon."

"You can't do this," Janel yelled. "You're ruining everything." She beat his chest with her free arm.

Hodgins kicked the gun away before grabbing her flailing arm. He couldn't simply throw her to the floor and risk harming the unborn child. He looked around, searching for the twine she used on the boxes. Distracted, he didn't see her bring back her leg.

"Damn."

Janel kicked his shin. Hodgins loosened his grip. It was just enough for her to break free. She shoved him, knocking him into a chair then ran down the hall and out the back door.

Hodgins didn't think she'd get far as she only wore

house shoes and didn't have a coat or shawl. He limped down the hall and looked out the still open door. A trail of footprints headed north. The second baby began crying. He couldn't leave them alone. The snow would reveal Janel's hiding place, so he hurried next door to fetch the neighbour to watch the twins.

Hodgins tracked Janel through her yard and onto a neighbouring lot. Her footprints disappeared around the corner of a house. He followed and found himself on Wellington Street. The area was covered in tracks, making it impossible to tell which way she went. Hodgins turned west, hoping Janel went towards the main part of town. He only got a few feet when he heard yelling. It sounded like, "get out of my yard." Hoping it was Janel, he crossed the road and headed toward where he thought the voice came from.

A few houses down he spotted tracks leading around a house. He heard someone pleading for help. Janel. Hodgins rounded the back of the house just as she was being allowed in.

"Stop. Toronto Constabulary." Hodgins ran to the door. Janel tried to push her way into the house, but the lady blocked her way.

"Don't want any bother with the law." She backed into her house, closing the door, leaving Janel out in the cold.

Janel dropped to her knees, shivering, cradling her belly. "Please, don't let anything happen to my baby."

Hodgins removed his overcoat and draped it over her shoulders, then led her to the train station. He gave a quick explanation to the station agent, who locked her in his office. Hodgins wired his station, then went back to the Brown's home to fetch a coat for Janel and ask the neighbour to mind the babies until someone came for them.

* * *

When the train arrived back in Toronto, Janel was taken to the hospital, a constable left guarding her door. She wasn't outside long enough to get frostbite, but the doctor wanted to keep her a day or two, just to make sure the baby was unharmed.

Hodgins hung his overcoat on a peg by the front door and joined his family in the kitchen to fill them in. "Well, I'm glad that's over with." Jonathan rubbed his throat. "I was beginning to feel the rope around my neck. I'd still like those boxing lessons, though."

Elizabeth rushed over to Hodgins and threw her arms around him. "Thank you Albert. I'm so relieved." She kissed his cheek then stood beside her husband. "We discussed it last night. As soon as Jonathan testifies we're going to sell the house and move here."

"I told her the children can stay here and get settled into school permanently," Cordelia said. "I know I should have spoken to you first, but I didn't think you'd mind."

"Of course they can stay here. Probably best if they're not around during the trial." He turned to Elizabeth. "You can wire the school tomorrow to have their records transferred."

Elizabeth looped her arm through her husband's. "Jonathan, maybe we can start looking around after Christmas for a suitable location for you to start over? Might be able to get you set up by February. House too."

Jonathan looked out the kitchen window at the children playing in the back with Scraps. "Maybe a dog as well?"

"One thing at a time dear. I'm sure Sara will share for awhile." Elizabeth peered over his shoulder. "Wherever would we find another dog like Scraps anyway?"

"As you said, one thing at a time." Delia reached for Elizabeth's hand. "This Christmas is going to be extra special. Come, let's start planning the Christmas Eve party."

CHAPTER TWENTY-TWO

The next three days exhausted everyone as they hurried to finish all the preparations for the party. Sara and Cora made the invitations and personally delivered them. Every room on the main floor had been decorated and was ready to be filled with family and friends. Cordelia's mother would make the plum pudding and mince pies, which would be warming on the wood stove while they consumed their main meal. Elizabeth prepared a large bowl of chestnut stuffing, while Cordelia took care of the roast goose. Along with the goose, they'd also have cold sliced roast beef and chicken, apples, oranges, boiled potatoes, and wine.

Sara and Cora wanted to make gilded walnut, raisin, and nut garlands, as well as popcorn balls for the tree and hallway. Since they were having a party, Cordelia agreed and added the necessary items to her shopping list. Once the girls had used all their supplies, they started baking sugar cookies and sweets. Freddie's job was to keep Scraps out of the way. He didn't need to be asked twice to play with the dog, especially as they let him test the cookies.

The day before the party Albert went to his in-laws and, with the help of Cordelia's father, brought over the pianoforte. Its rectangular shape fit perfectly between the fireplace and the Christmas tree. The little pale-blue piano had tiny pink and yellow roses painted along the top, connected with vines. A wreath had been painted in the centre of the music holder. Hodgins knew Delia missed being able to play whenever she wanted now that they weren't living with her parents. Maybe he'd look for one after his brother and family were settled.

Constable Barnes arrived late-afternoon with his mother and younger sister. His sweetheart Violet Halloday and her parents arrived shortly afterwards. As soon as Barnes introduced his family to Jonathan's he scampered across the room to be with Violet. Hodgins watched as Barnes slipped his arm around her waist. He figured they'd be married by spring, and knew another party in his home was inevitable.

Despite Hodgins' best efforts, talk soon turned to the recent murders.

"Imagine," Cordelia's mother said. "A young woman having her husband murdered just so she could be with her fancy man. And to frame Jonathan for it. Disgraceful, not to mention those two babies and another on the way.

Any idea what will happen to them?"

"She'll remain in jail until her baby comes, then it will be put up for adoption. Normally, she'd hang for her part in the killings, but she's given us the name of the man she hired. I expect the judge will give her life in prison instead, Hodgins said.

"Her twins have already been taken to the St. Paul's House of Providence. Most likely they'll be parceled out separately. Not many would welcome two little ones at once." Barnes shook his head. "Imagine. Having a sister and never knowing it."

"I think we should take them, Daddy." Everyone turned to Sara. "I wish I had a sister. I was ever so sad when Mommy lost the baby."

"Heavens, you remember that?" Cordelia asked. "You were only five."

"Oh, please, can we have the babies? I'm old enough to help take care of them."

The guests all remained silent, enjoying the unexpected conversation.

Hodgins and Cordelia exchanged a look. Cordelia smiled. "Your father and I will have to discuss it Sara."

"Cordelia, how can you consider such a thing?" her mother asked. "The babies of a murderess?"

Sara squealed and clapped her hands. "Oh, please,

Daddy? Babies for Christmas. I already know what we can name them. Holly and Ivy."

"As your mother said, we'll have to discuss it." He winked at Cordelia before turning back to Sara. "Why, they may not think us suitable parents after they see how we've raised you."

Mr. Halloday cleared his throat. "I've a sort of announcement to make myself. I say, I'd like to make an announcement."

Hodgins turned towards Barnes, thinking the young constable couldn't wait and he'd already asked for Violet's hand. Barnes shrugged in answer to the unspoken question.

"I've been in correspondence with my sister. She's planning a tour of Europe in the New Year and I've arranged for my daughter, Violet, to accompany her. They'll be gone four, maybe five months. Splendid opportunity for her to learn art and culture from several different countries. Rub elbows with the higher echelon. My sister is acquainted with many high-ranking people abroad."

"F-f-f-five months?" If at all possible, Barnes' jaw would have landed on the hardwood floor. He moved across the room and stood beside the detective, whispering. "I can't ask her to marry me now. What if she meets a count or something?"

Before Hodgins could reply, Violet rushed over. "Oh, Henry. Isn't this the most exciting news? London, Paris, maybe even Cairo. All those magnificent art galleries." She stopped as she noticed the look on his face.

Hodgins watched in amusement. Her expression changed continually as she worked things out in her mind. Finally, her eyes widened, the joyful look gone.

"Henry! I promise, I'll be absolutely miserable without you. It will feel like years. I wish you could see it all with me."

Barnes tried to smile. "No, you'll enjoy your adventure. I forbid you to be miserable. Promise you'll write often."

"Every day. I promise."

While the young couple discussed the next several months, Hodgins wove his way through the crowd to the sitting room doorway and took the tray of sweets from Cordelia.

"Poor Henry." Cordelia tsked and shook her head. "Mrs. Halloday was telling me just the other day about her sister-in-law's trip. Now I understand her comment about eligible young noblemen. How could they even think about sending her away to find a husband when they know how much in love those two are? I thought they liked

Henry."

"Poor Henry indeed. He asked me not to say anything, but he was planning on proposing after Christmas. He just told me he won't now. He's going to be a bugger to work with until she returns. For his sake, she'd better come back without a count in tow."

Hodgins put the tray on the side table and they re-joined their guests, now crowded around the pianoforte. His mother-in-law played Silent Night while Barnes stood by the crackling fire, alone.

ABOUT THE AUTHOR

Nanci M. Pattenden is a genealogist and an emerging fiction writer, currently working on a collection of detective stories set in Victorian Toronto.

She has completed the Creative Writing program at both the University of Calgary and the University of Toronto.

Nanci currently resides in Newmarket with her fluffy cat Snowball.

nanci@nancipattenden.com
www.murderdoespayink.ca
www.nancipattenden.com
@npattenden